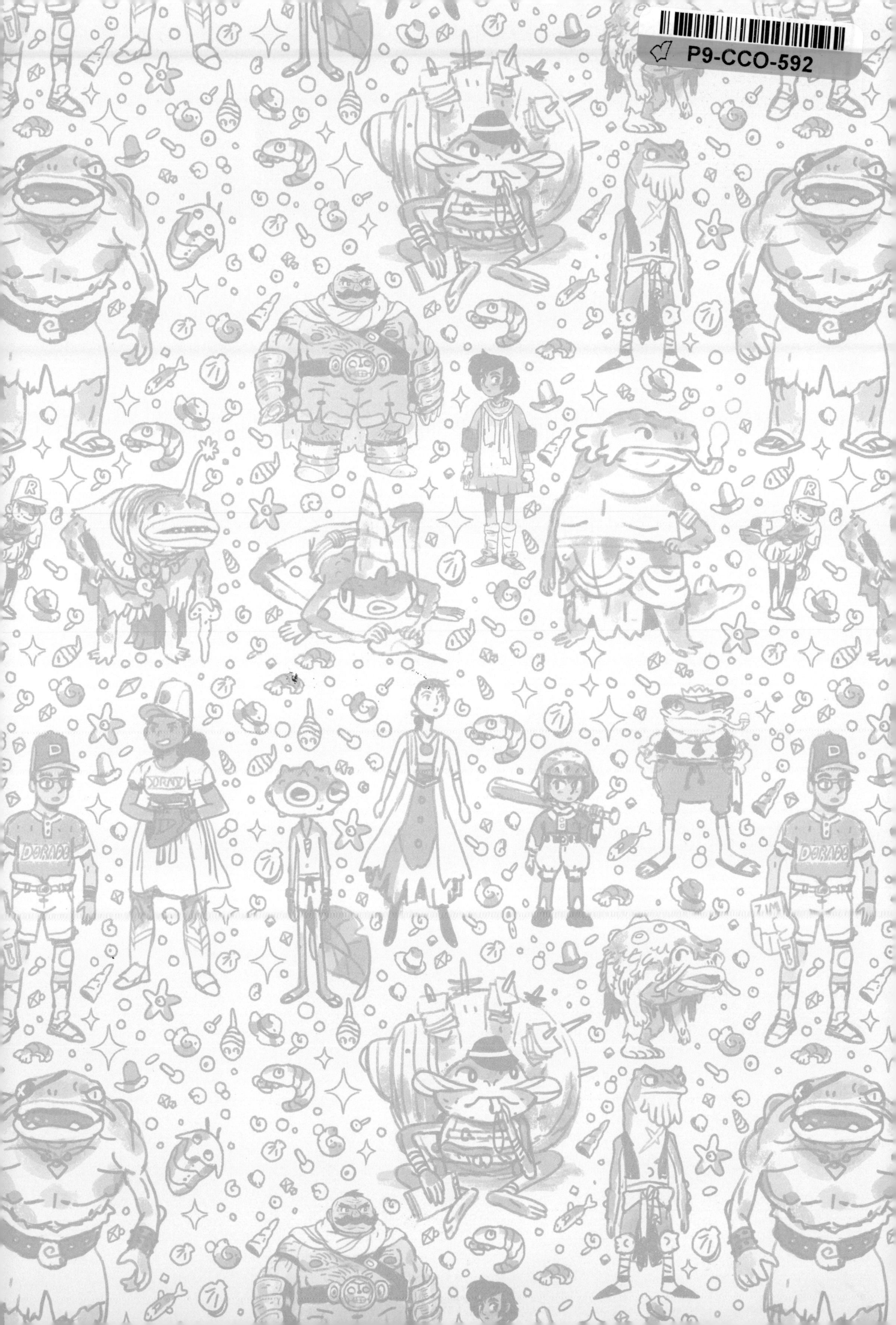
DORADO

AM BOSMA

FANTASY SPORTS

NO. 2

THE BANDIT OF BARBEL BAY

NOBROW
LONDON – NEW YORK

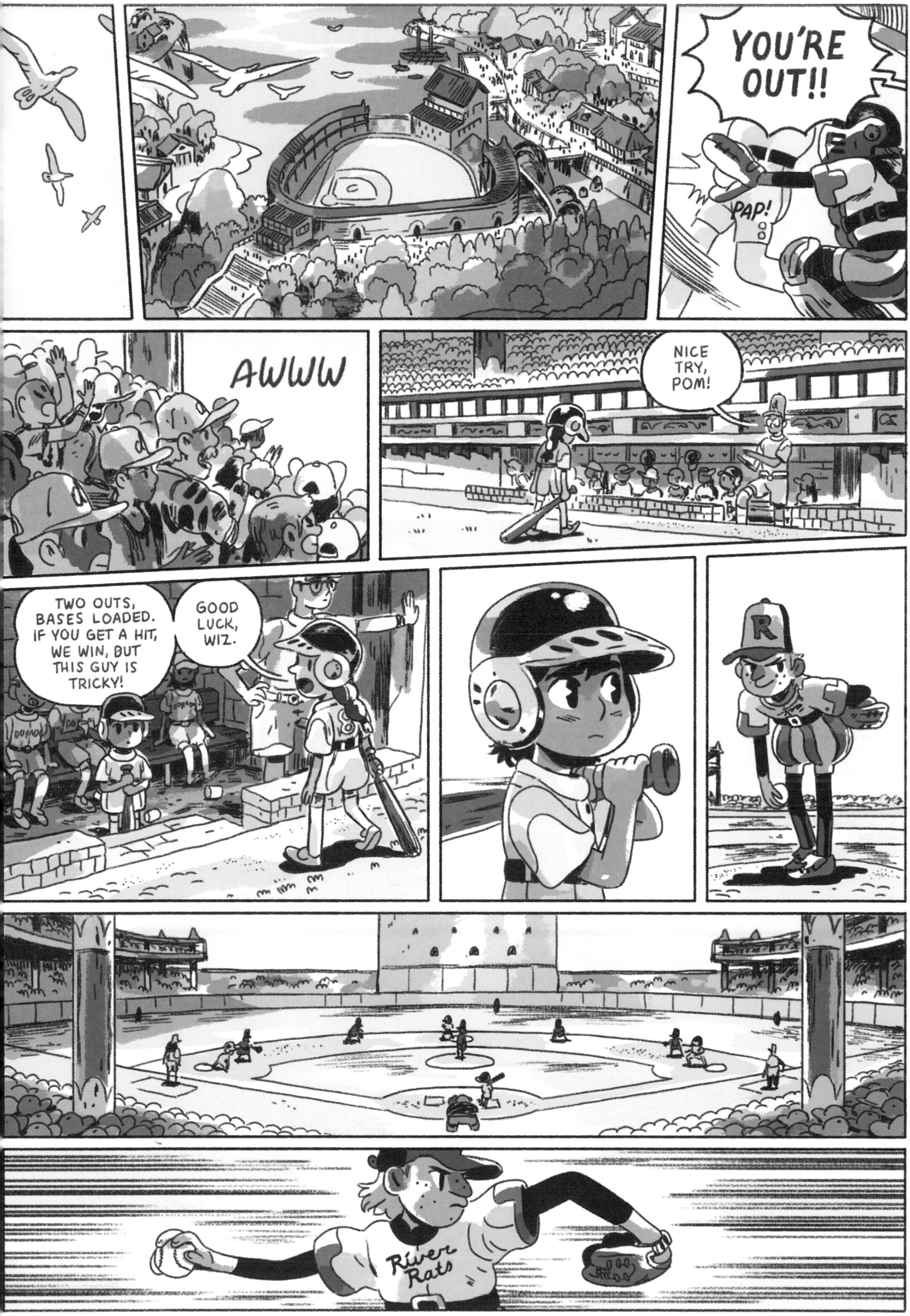
YOU'RE OUT!!
PAP!
AWWW
NICE TRY, POM!
TWO OUTS, BASES LOADED. IF YOU GET A HIT, WE WIN, BUT THIS GUY IS TRICKY!
GOOD LUCK, WIZ.
River Rats

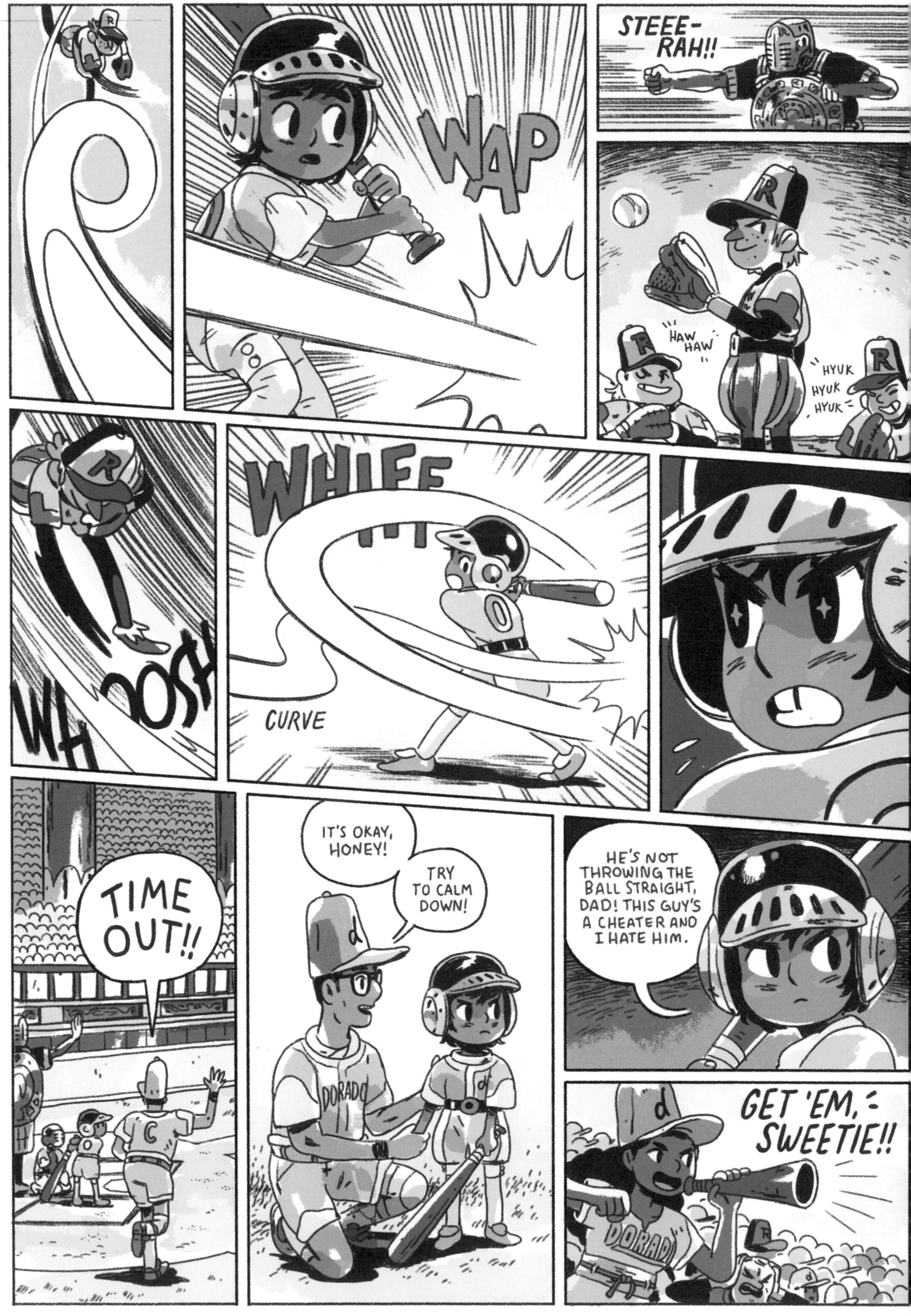

WAP
STEEE-RAH!!
HAW HAW
HYUK HYUK HYUK
WHOOSH
WHIFF
CURVE
TIME OUT!!
IT'S OKAY, HONEY!
TRY TO CALM DOWN!
HE'S NOT THROWING THE BALL STRAIGHT, DAD! THIS GUY'S A CHEATER AND I HATE HIM.
GET 'EM, SWEETIE!!

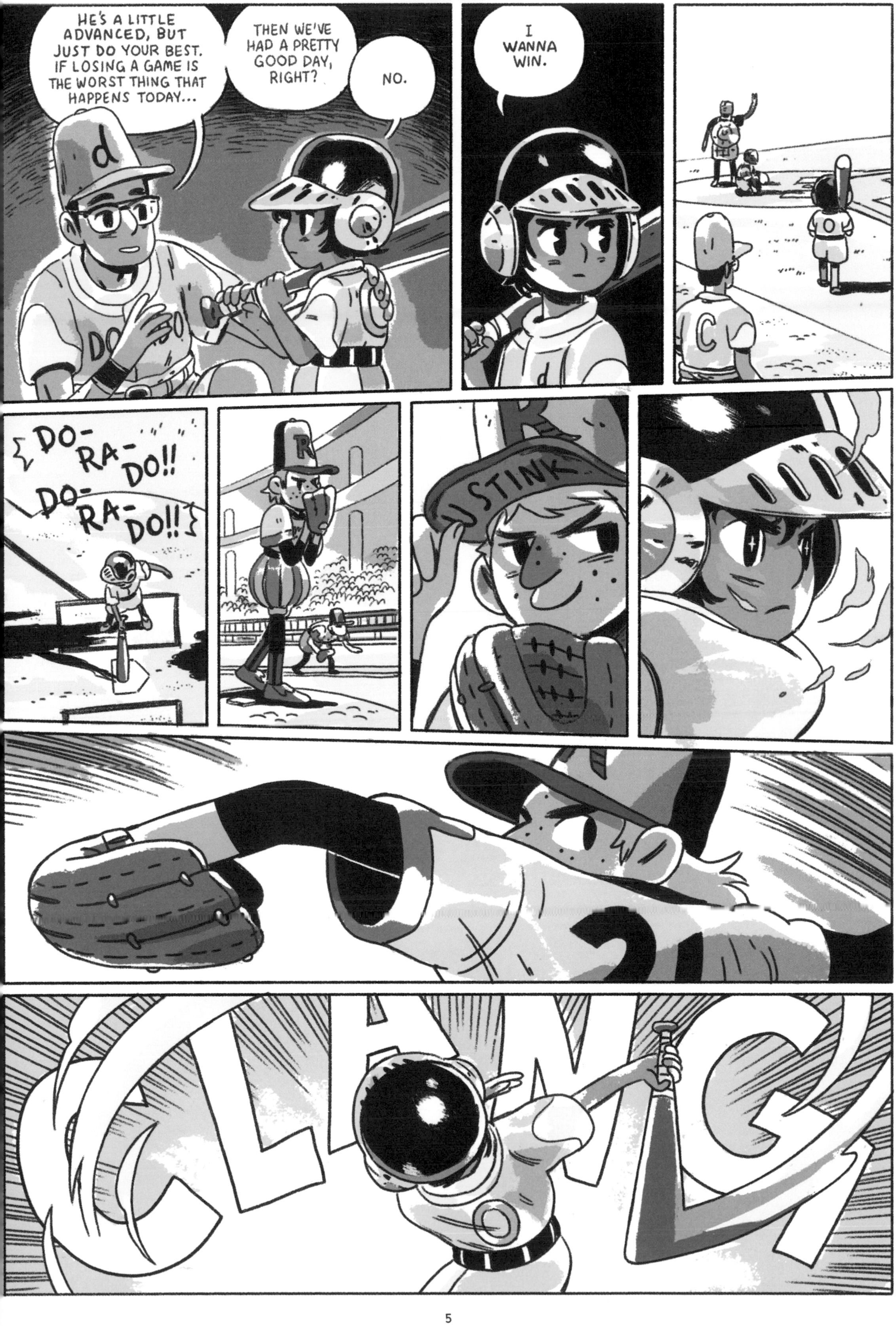
HE'S A LITTLE ADVANCED, BUT JUST DO YOUR BEST. IF LOSING A GAME IS THE WORST THING THAT HAPPENS TODAY...
THEN WE'VE HAD A PRETTY GOOD DAY, RIGHT?
NO.
I WANNA WIN.
DO-RA-DO!! DO-RA-DO!!
STINK
CLANG

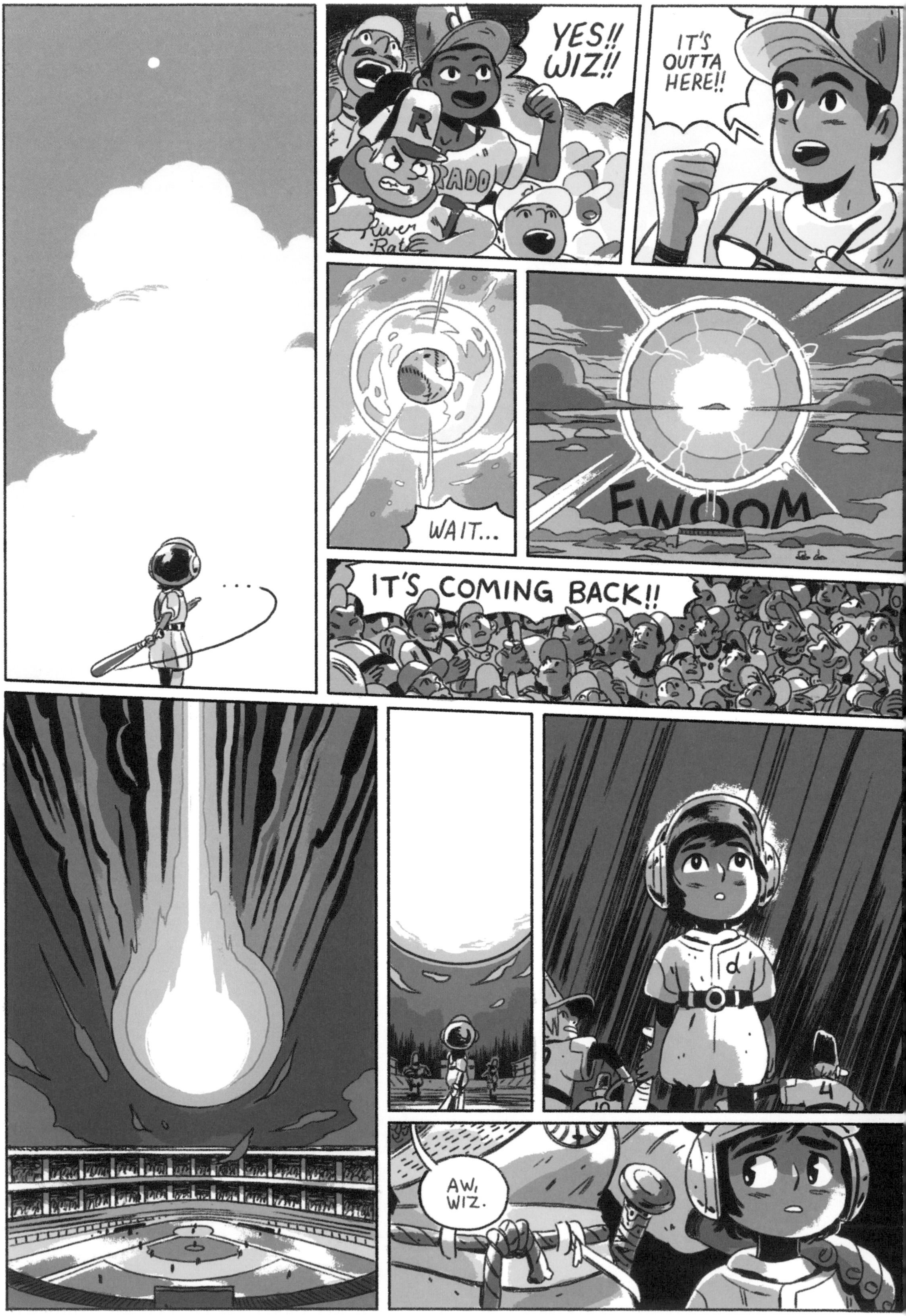
...
YES!! WIZ!!
RADO
River Rats
IT'S OUTTA HERE!!
WAIT...
FWOOM
IT'S COMING BACK!!
AW, WIZ.

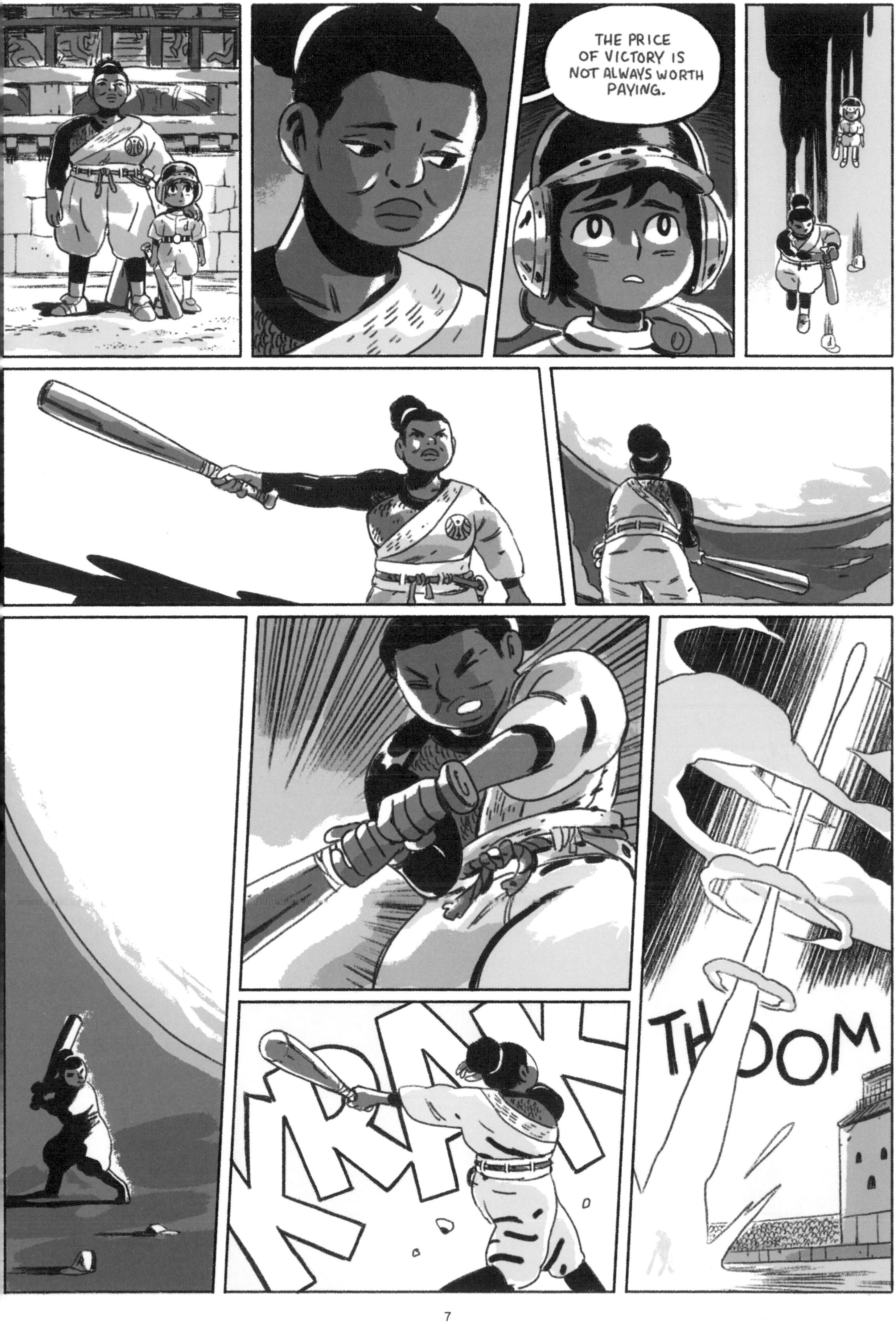
THE PRICE OF VICTORY IS NOT ALWAYS WORTH PAYING.
THOOM

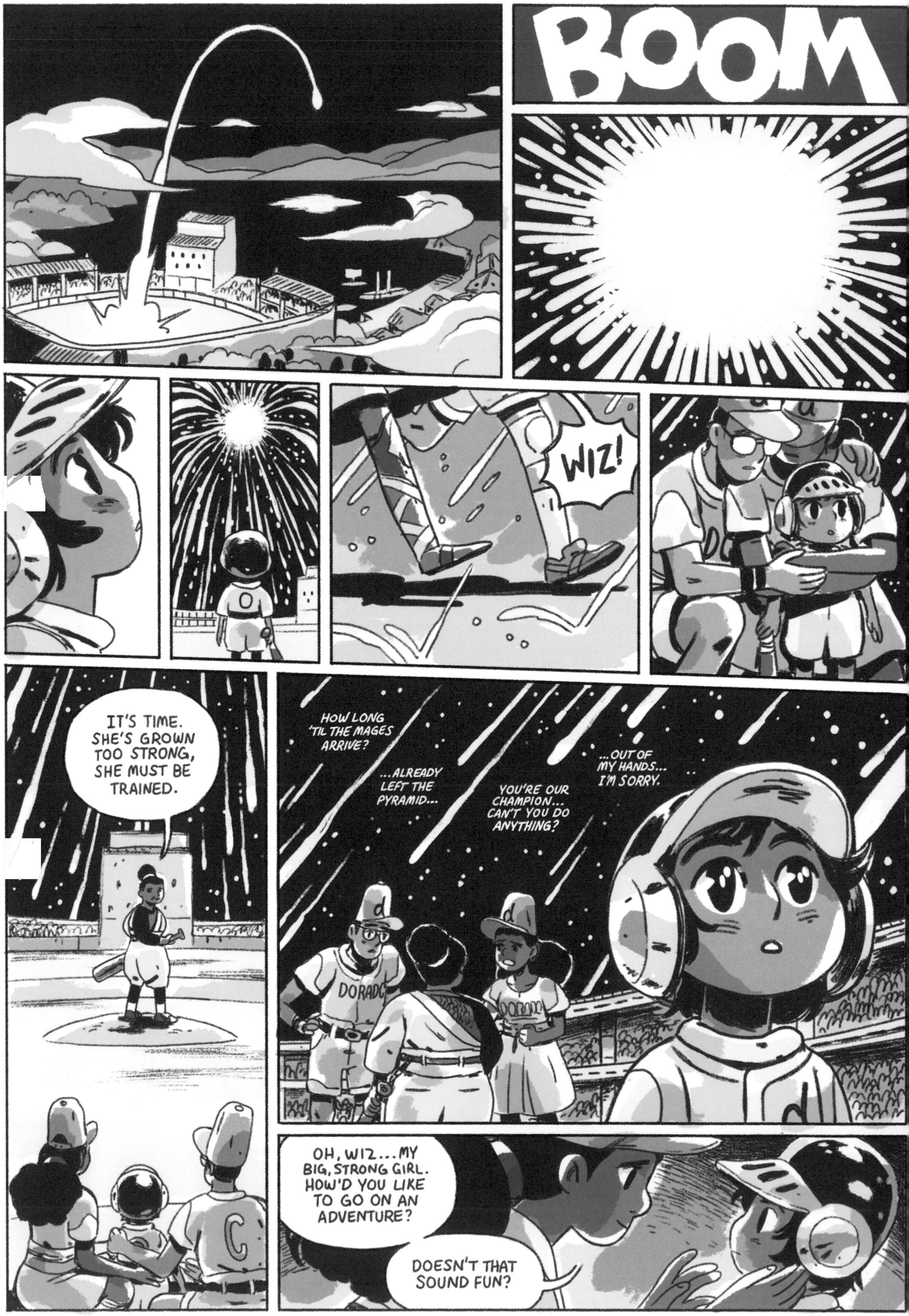
BOOM
WIZ!
IT'S TIME. SHE'S GROWN TOO STRONG, SHE MUST BE TRAINED.
HOW LONG 'TIL THE MAGES ARRIVE?
...ALREADY LEFT THE PYRAMID...
YOU'RE OUR CHAMPION... CAN'T YOU DO ANYTHING?
...OUT OF MY HANDS... I'M SORRY.
OH, WIZ... MY BIG, STRONG GIRL. HOW'D YOU LIKE TO GO ON AN ADVENTURE?
DOESN'T THAT SOUND FUN?

PUH

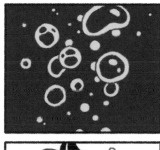

OH, NO.
NOT GOOD.

WE'RE SUPPOSED TO BE BACK AT THE PYRAMID! WHERE ARE WE?!

LOOKS LIKE THE OCEAN, KID.

HMM... BUT WHICH OCEAN?

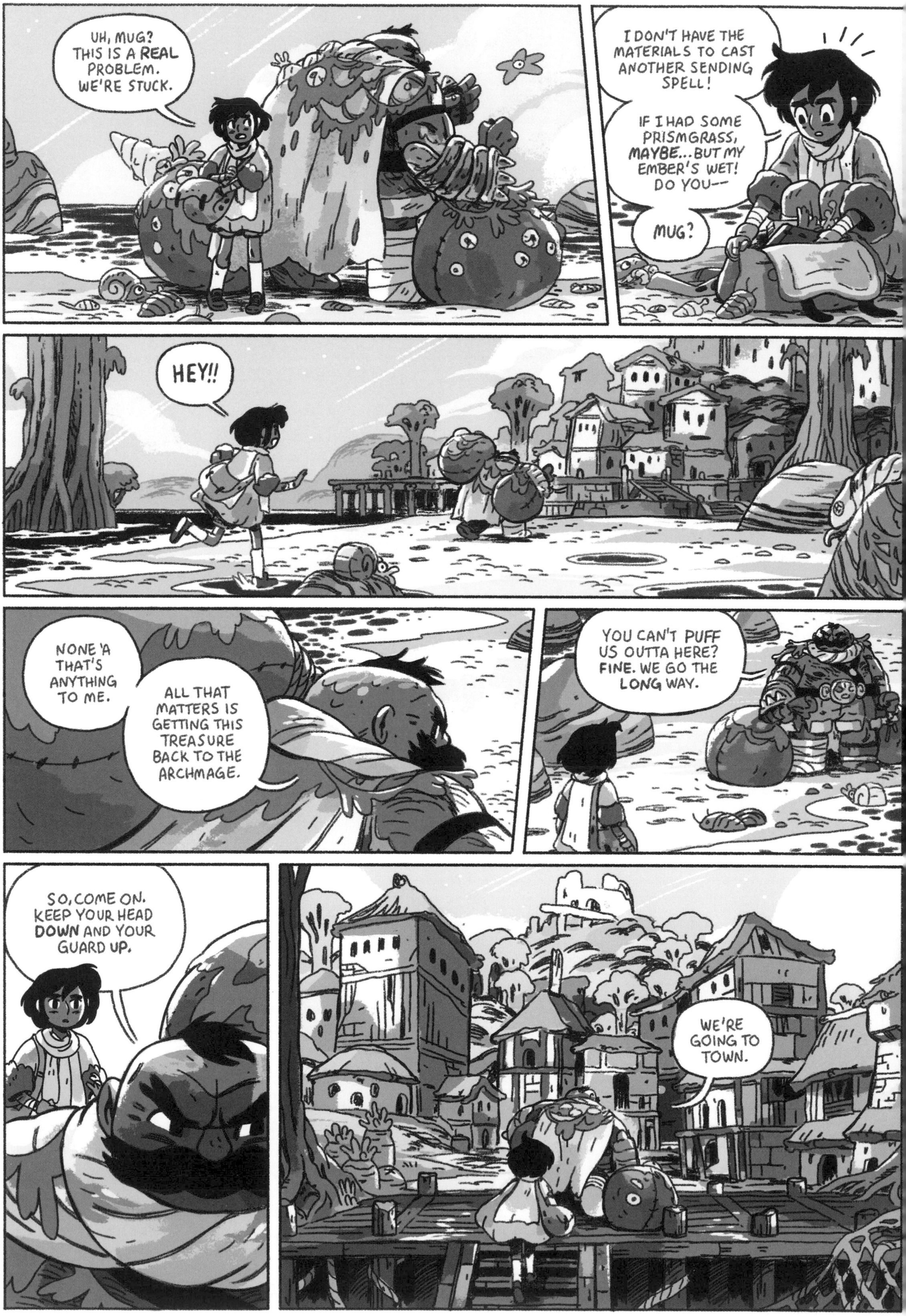
UH, MUG? THIS IS A REAL PROBLEM. WE'RE STUCK.
I DON'T HAVE THE MATERIALS TO CAST ANOTHER SENDING SPELL!
IF I HAD SOME PRISMGRASS, MAYBE... BUT MY EMBER'S WET! DO YOU--
MUG?
HEY!!
NONE 'A THAT'S ANYTHING TO ME.
ALL THAT MATTERS IS GETTING THIS TREASURE BACK TO THE ARCHMAGE.
YOU CAN'T PUFF US OUTTA HERE? FINE. WE GO THE LONG WAY.
SO, COME ON. KEEP YOUR HEAD DOWN AND YOUR GUARD UP.
WE'RE GOING TO TOWN.

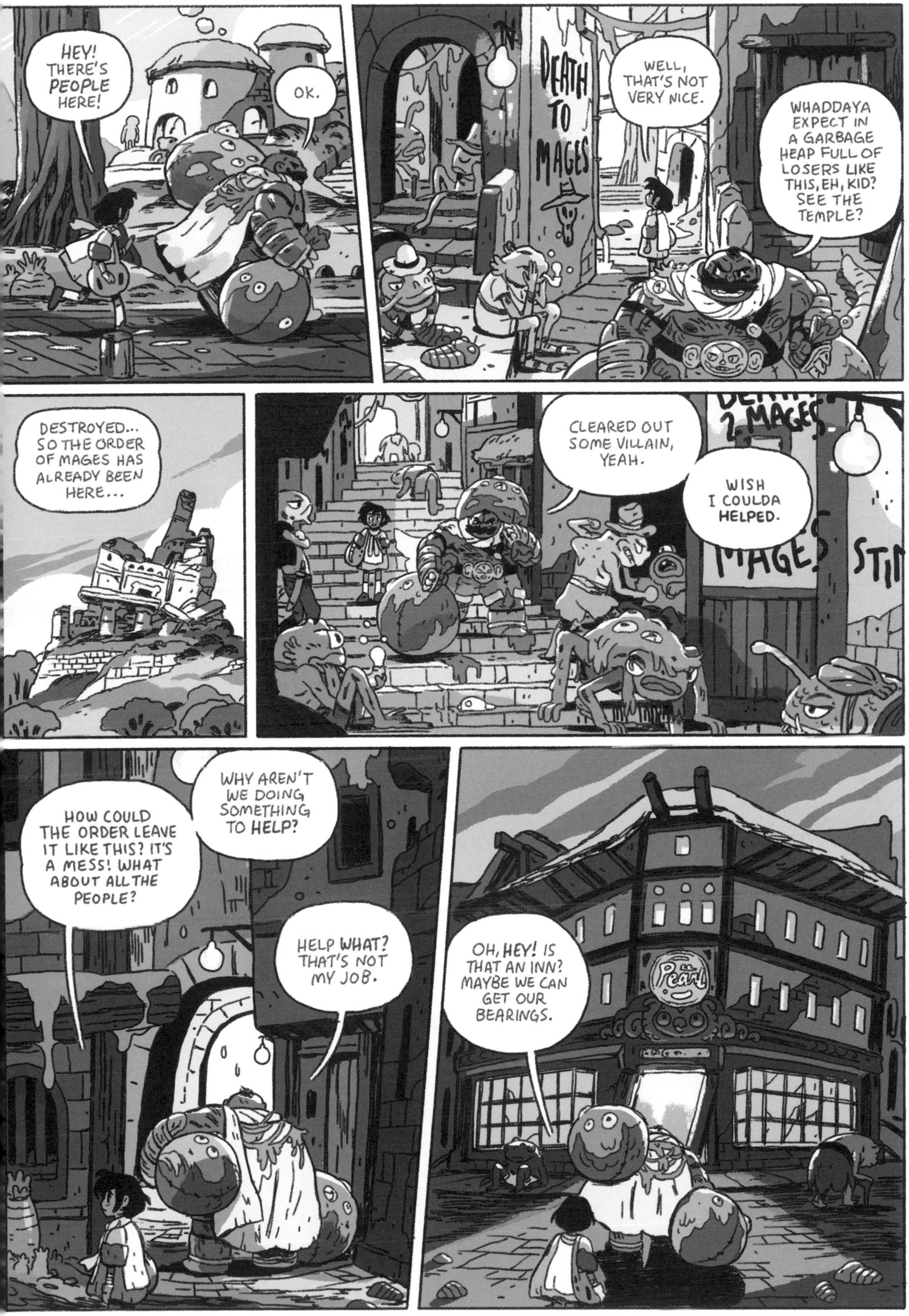
HEY! THERE'S PEOPLE HERE!
OK.
DEATH TO MAGES
WELL, THAT'S NOT VERY NICE.
WHADDAYA EXPECT IN A GARBAGE HEAP FULL OF LOSERS LIKE THIS, EH, KID? SEE THE TEMPLE?
DESTROYED... SO THE ORDER OF MAGES HAS ALREADY BEEN HERE...
CLEARED OUT SOME VILLAIN, YEAH.
WISH I COULDA HELPED.
HOW COULD THE ORDER LEAVE IT LIKE THIS? IT'S A MESS! WHAT ABOUT ALL THE PEOPLE?
WHY AREN'T WE DOING SOMETHING TO HELP?
HELP WHAT? THAT'S NOT MY JOB.
OH, HEY! IS THAT AN INN? MAYBE WE CAN GET OUR BEARINGS.
Pearl

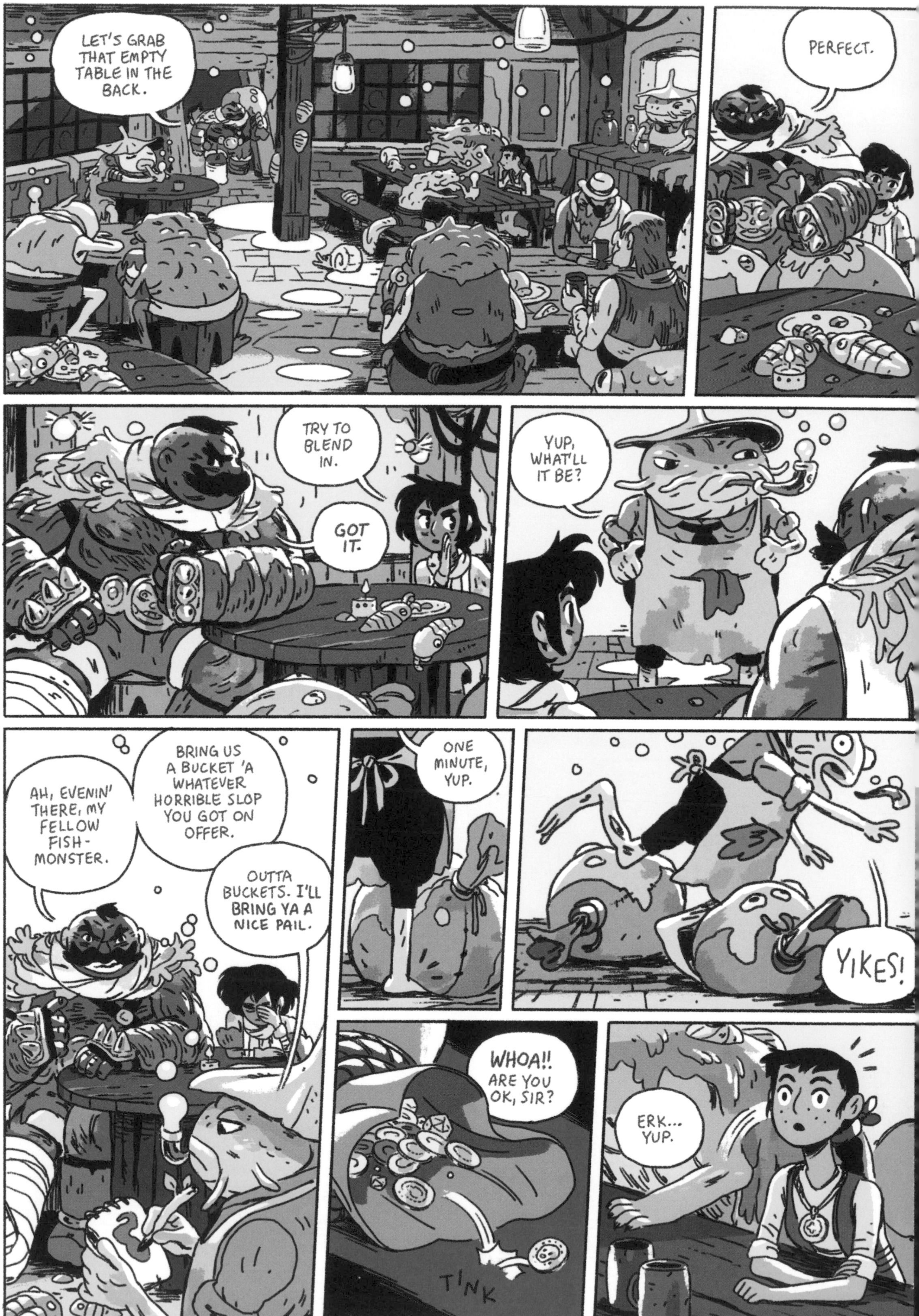
LET'S GRAB THAT EMPTY TABLE IN THE BACK.
PERFECT.
TRY TO BLEND IN.
GOT IT.
YUP, WHAT'LL IT BE?
AH, EVENIN' THERE, MY FELLOW FISH-MONSTER.
BRING US A BUCKET 'A WHATEVER HORRIBLE SLOP YOU GOT ON OFFER.
OUTTA BUCKETS. I'LL BRING YA A NICE PAIL.
ONE MINUTE, YUP.
YIKES!
WHOA!! ARE YOU OK, SIR?
TINK
ERK... YUP.

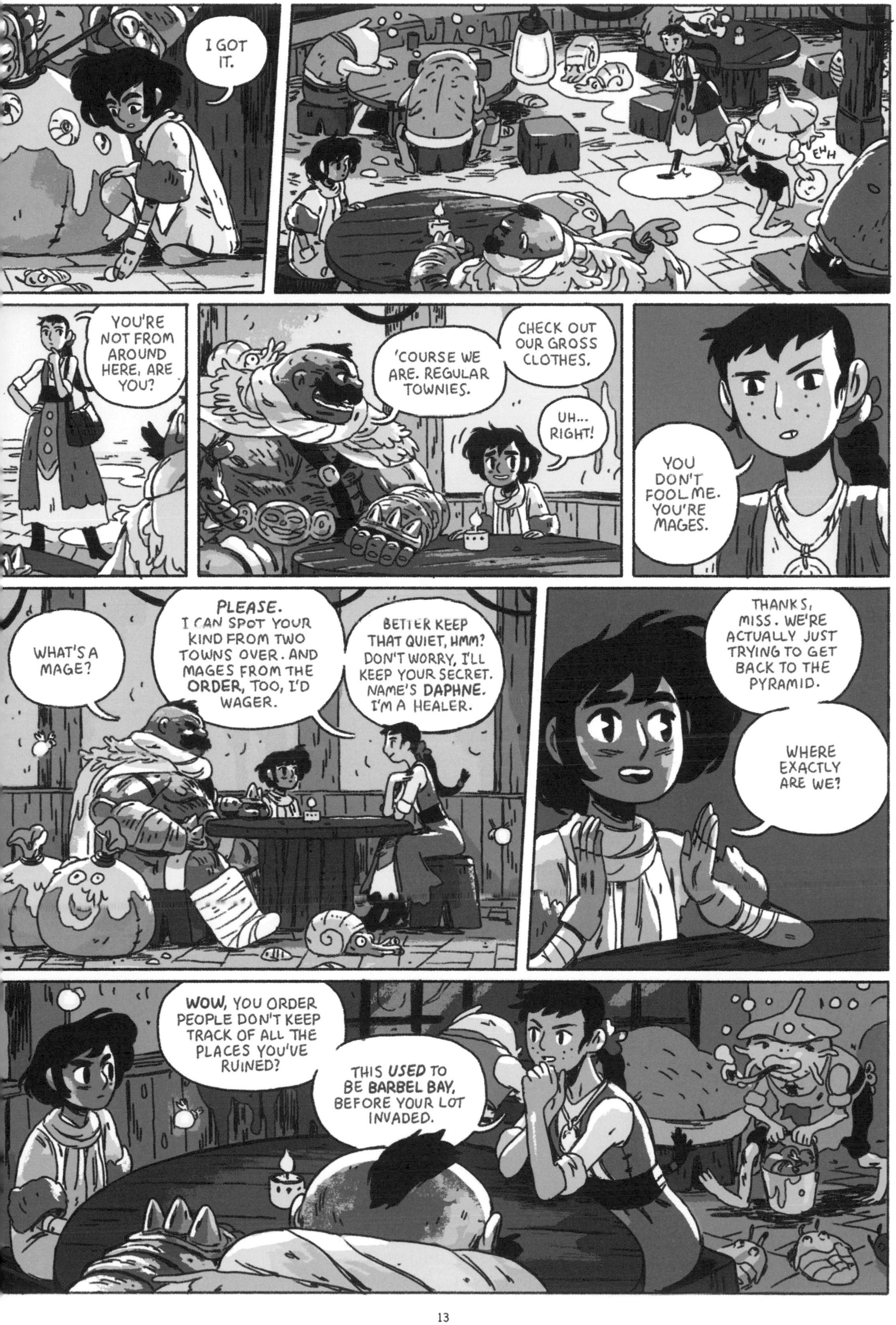
I GOT IT.
EHH
YOU'RE NOT FROM AROUND HERE, ARE YOU?
'COURSE WE ARE. REGULAR TOWNIES.
CHECK OUT OUR GROSS CLOTHES.
UH... RIGHT!
YOU DON'T FOOL ME. YOU'RE MAGES.
WHAT'S A MAGE?
PLEASE. I CAN SPOT YOUR KIND FROM TWO TOWNS OVER. AND MAGES FROM THE ORDER, TOO, I'D WAGER.
BETTER KEEP THAT QUIET, HMM? DON'T WORRY, I'LL KEEP YOUR SECRET. NAME'S DAPHNE. I'M A HEALER.
THANKS, MISS. WE'RE ACTUALLY JUST TRYING TO GET BACK TO THE PYRAMID.
WHERE EXACTLY ARE WE?
WOW, YOU ORDER PEOPLE DON'T KEEP TRACK OF ALL THE PLACES YOU'VE RUINED?
THIS USED TO BE BARBEL BAY, BEFORE YOUR LOT INVADED.

THAT'S WHAT HAPPENS WHEN A CHAMPION TURNS INTO A TYRANT. THE ORDER HAS TO INTERVENE.

THIS PLACE MUST'VE BEEN EVEN WORSE BEFORE THE ORDER GOT HERE.

OH BOY, THEY'VE GOT YOU TRAINED PRETTY GOOD, HUH?

WHAT'S *THAT* SUPPOSED TO MEAN?

MUNCH

CHOMP

BARBEL BAY WAS A NICE PLACE— FAIR CHAMPION, HAPPY PEOPLE, LOTS OF TREASURE. BUT THAT WAS BEFORE THE ORDER RAINED FIRE DOWN AND TOOK IT ALL AWAY.

I DON'T BELIEVE YOU.

EH, FORGET ALL 'A THAT.

YER A HEALER, YEAH? YOU FIX BUSTED LEGS?

URP

FOR A PRICE.

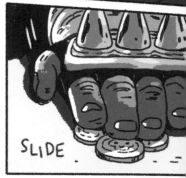

SLIDE

TAKE A ROOM HERE AND LIGHT THIS BEFORE YOU SLEEP. BY MORNING, YOU'LL BE FRESH AS A LILY.

A CANDLE. *SWELL.*

BLESSINGS BE UPON YOU.

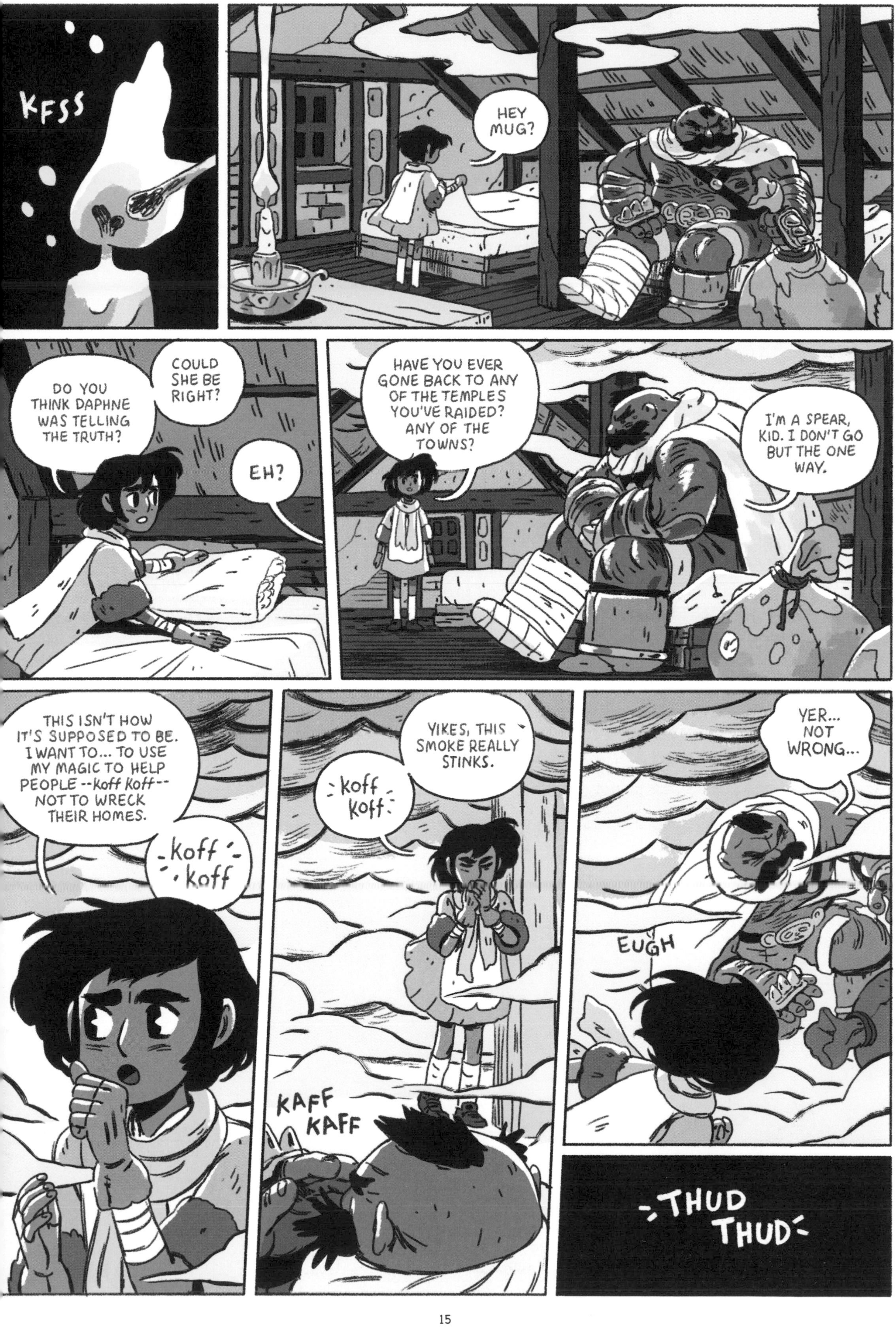
KFSS
HEY MUG?
DO YOU THINK DAPHNE WAS TELLING THE TRUTH?
COULD SHE BE RIGHT?
EH?
HAVE YOU EVER GONE BACK TO ANY OF THE TEMPLES YOU'VE RAIDED? ANY OF THE TOWNS?
I'M A SPEAR, KID. I DON'T GO BUT THE ONE WAY.
THIS ISN'T HOW IT'S SUPPOSED TO BE. I WANT TO... TO USE MY MAGIC TO HELP PEOPLE --koff koff-- NOT TO WRECK THEIR HOMES.
koff koff
YIKES, THIS SMOKE REALLY STINKS.
koff koff
KAFF KAFF
YER... NOT WRONG...
EUGH
THUD THUD

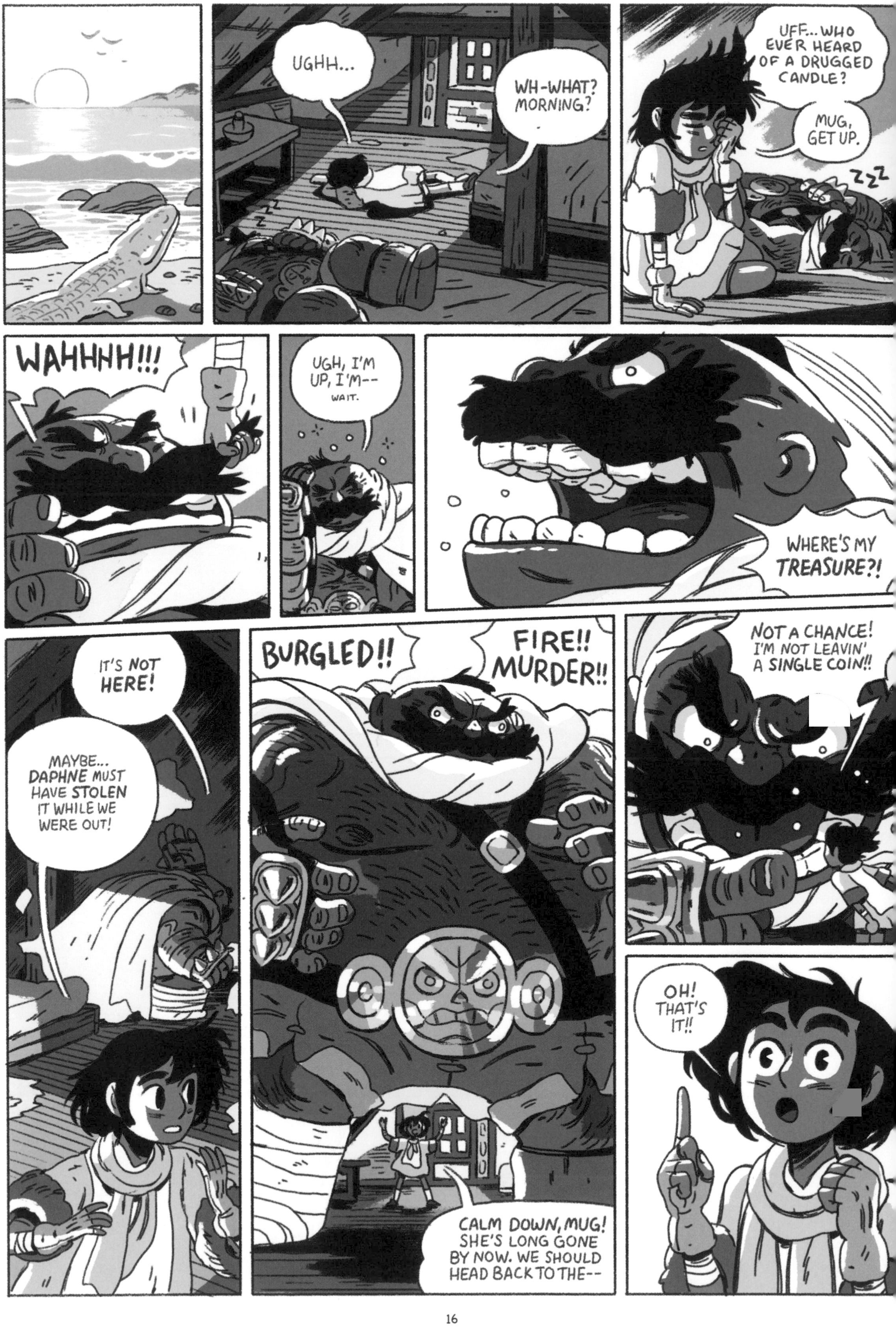
UGHH...
WH-WHAT? MORNING?
UFF... WHO EVER HEARD OF A DRUGGED CANDLE?
MUG, GET UP.
ZZZ
WAHHHH!!!
UGH, I'M UP, I'M-- WAIT.
WHERE'S MY TREASURE?!
IT'S NOT HERE!
MAYBE... DAPHNE MUST HAVE STOLEN IT WHILE WE WERE OUT!
BURGLED!!
FIRE!! MURDER!!
CALM DOWN, MUG! SHE'S LONG GONE BY NOW. WE SHOULD HEAD BACK TO THE--
NOT A CHANCE! I'M NOT LEAVIN' A SINGLE COIN!!
OH! THAT'S IT!!

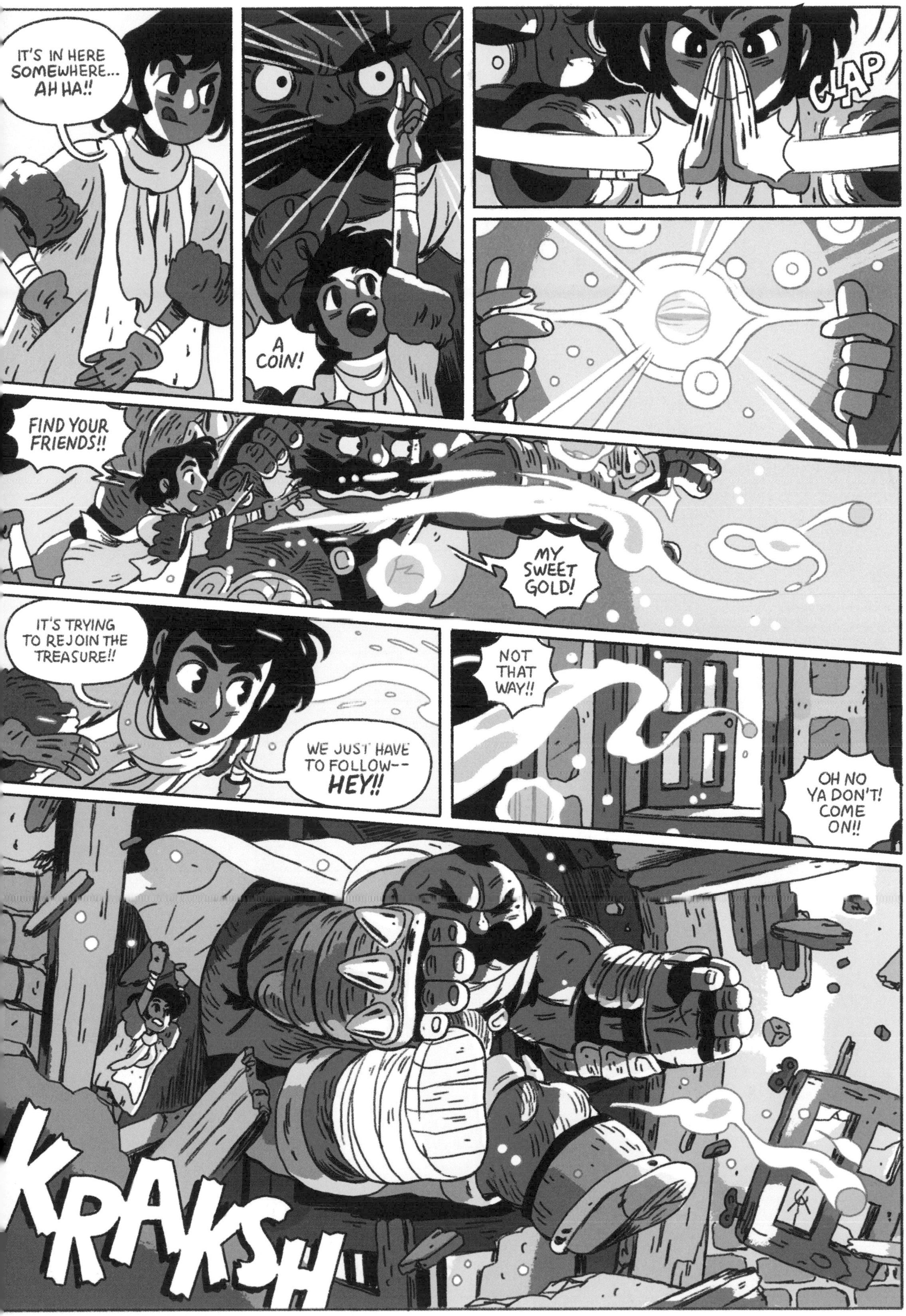
IT'S IN HERE SOMEWHERE... AH HA!!
A COIN!
CLAP
FIND YOUR FRIENDS!!
MY SWEET GOLD!
IT'S TRYING TO REJOIN THE TREASURE!!
WE JUST HAVE TO FOLLOW-- HEY!!
NOT THAT WAY!!
OH NO YA DON'T! COME ON!!
KRAKSH

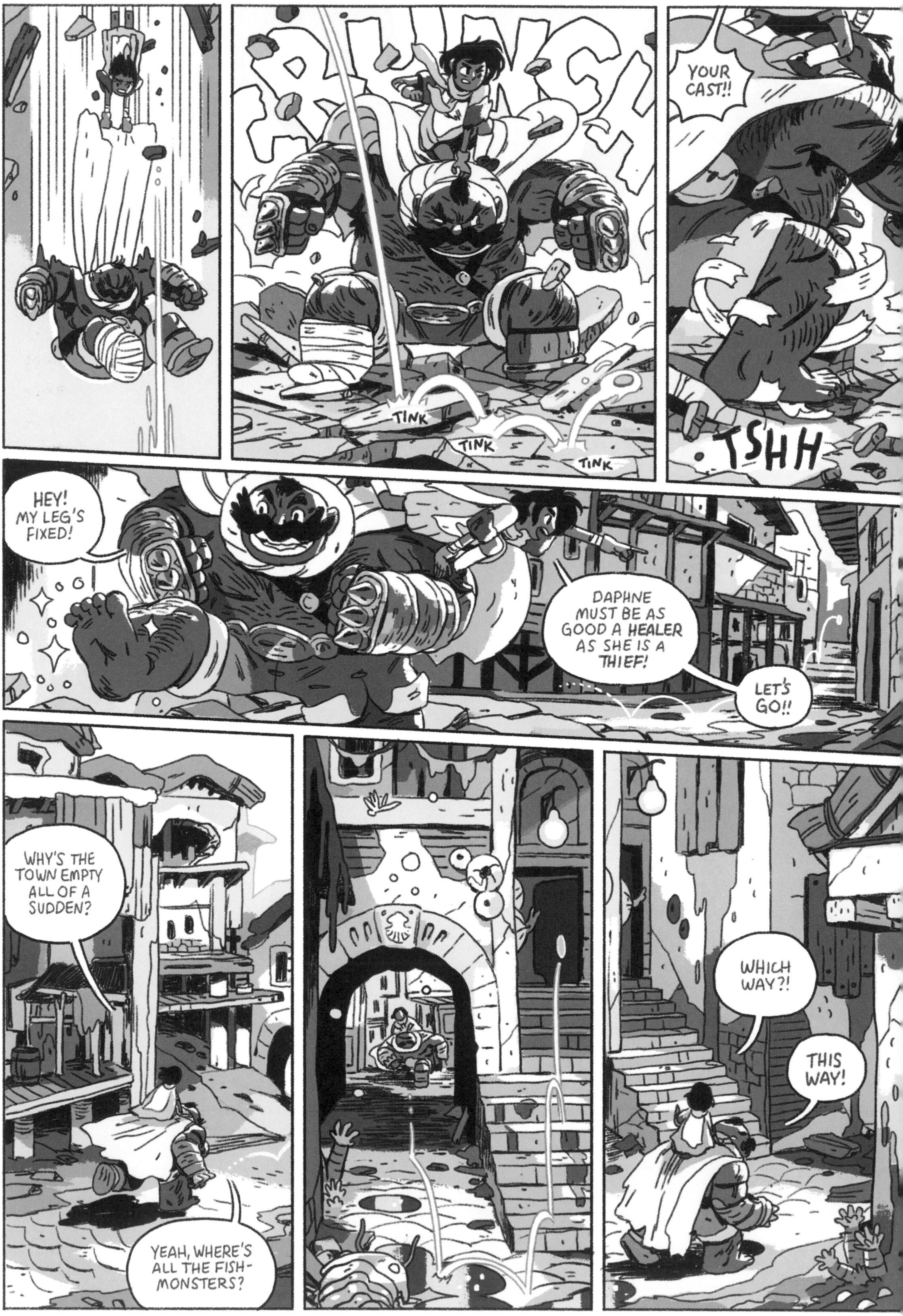
CRUNCH
TINK
TINK
TINK
YOUR CAST!!
TSHH
HEY! MY LEG'S FIXED!
DAPHNE MUST BE AS GOOD A HEALER AS SHE IS A THIEF!
LET'S GO!!
WHY'S THE TOWN EMPTY ALL OF A SUDDEN?
YEAH, WHERE'S ALL THE FISH-MONSTERS?
WHICH WAY?!
THIS WAY!

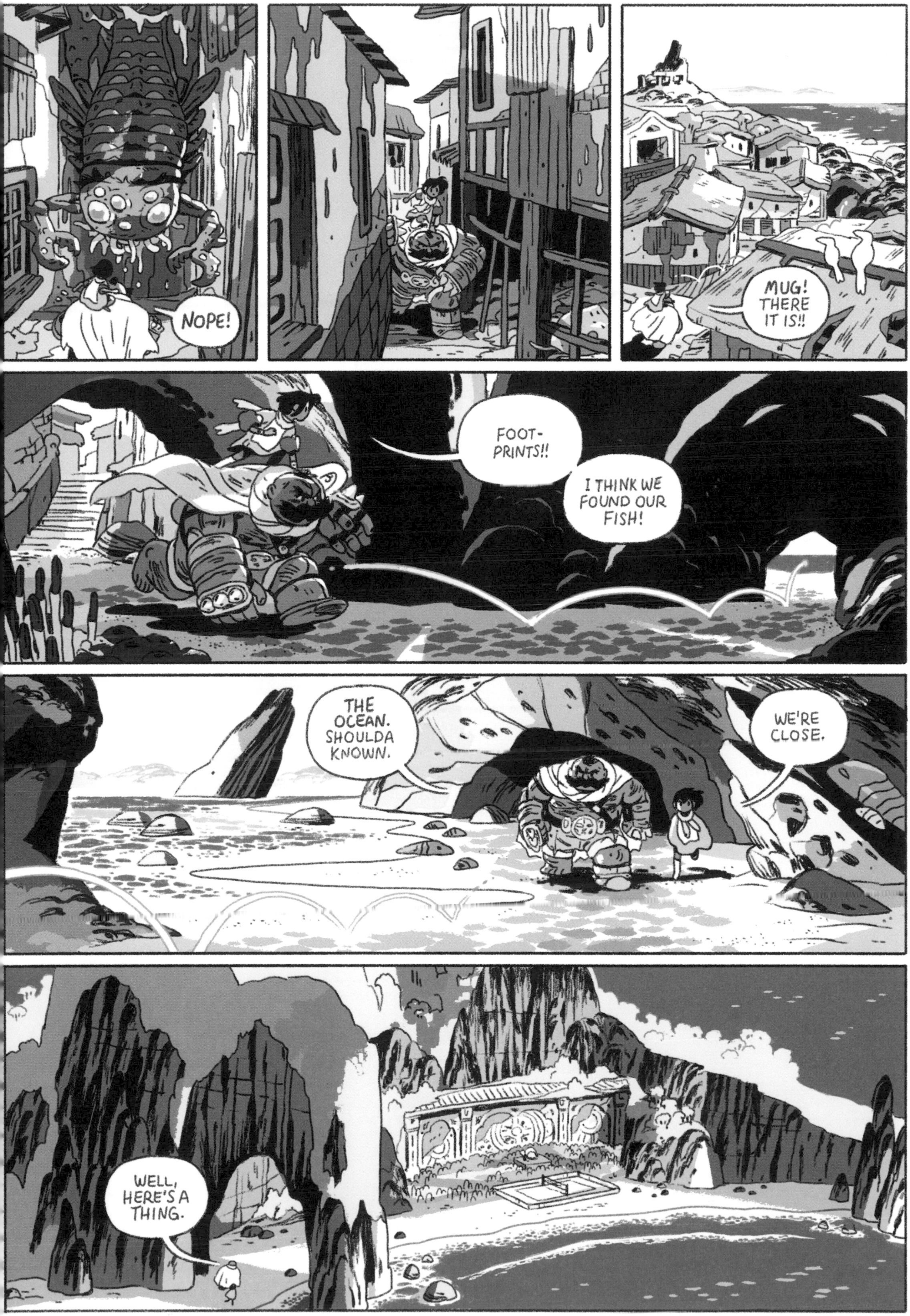
NOPE!
MUG! THERE IT IS!!
FOOT-PRINTS!!
I THINK WE FOUND OUR FISH!
THE OCEAN. SHOULDA KNOWN.
WE'RE CLOSE.
WELL, HERE'S A THING.

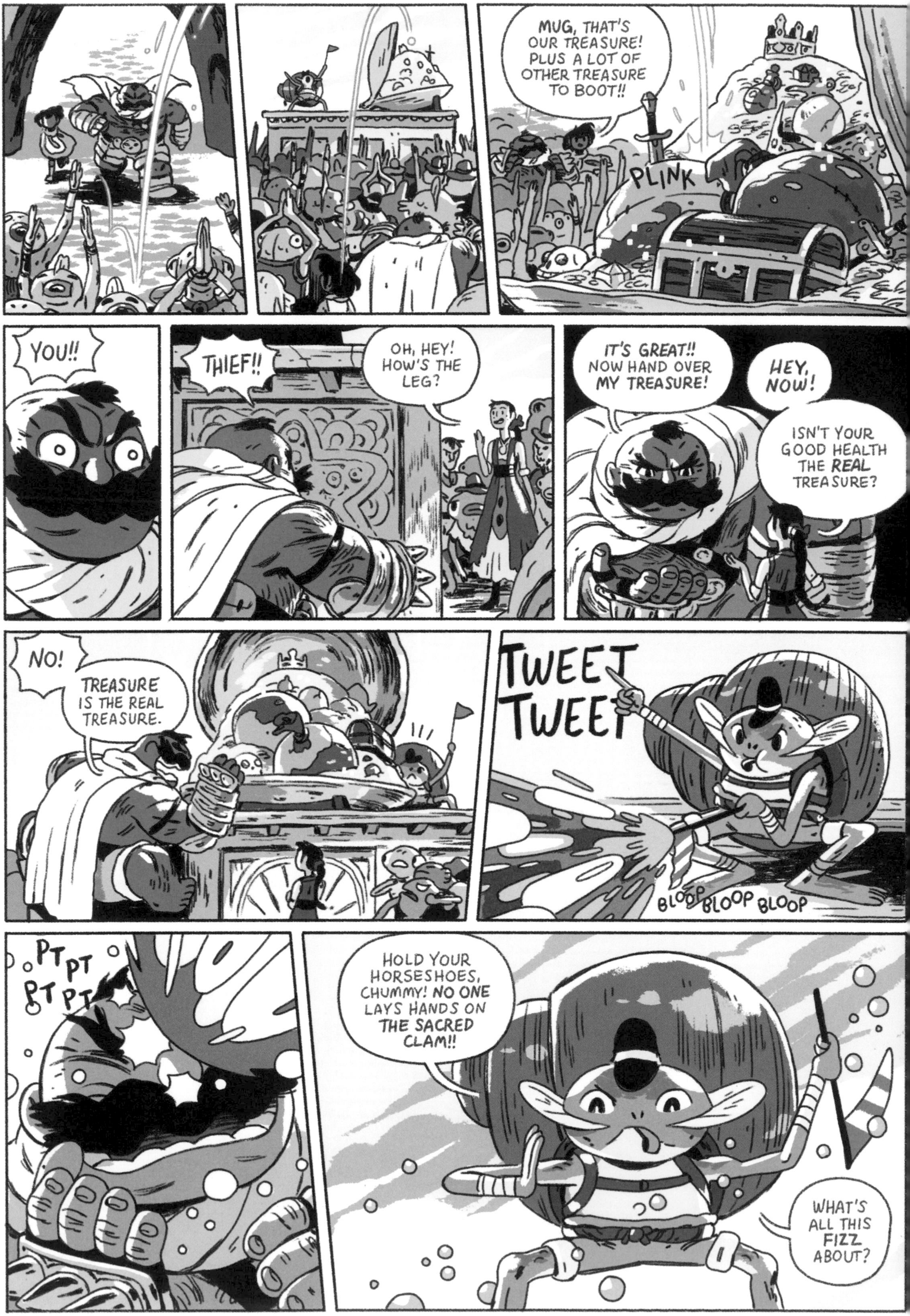

MUG, THAT'S OUR TREASURE! PLUS A LOT OF OTHER TREASURE TO BOOT!!
PLINK
YOU!!
THIEF!!
OH, HEY! HOW'S THE LEG?
IT'S GREAT!! NOW HAND OVER MY TREASURE!
HEY, NOW!
ISN'T YOUR GOOD HEALTH THE REAL TREASURE?
NO!
TREASURE IS THE REAL TREASURE.
TWEET TWEET
BLOOP BLOOP BLOOP
PT PT PT PT
HOLD YOUR HORSESHOES, CHUMMY! NO ONE LAYS HANDS ON THE SACRED CLAM!!
WHAT'S ALL THIS FIZZ ABOUT?

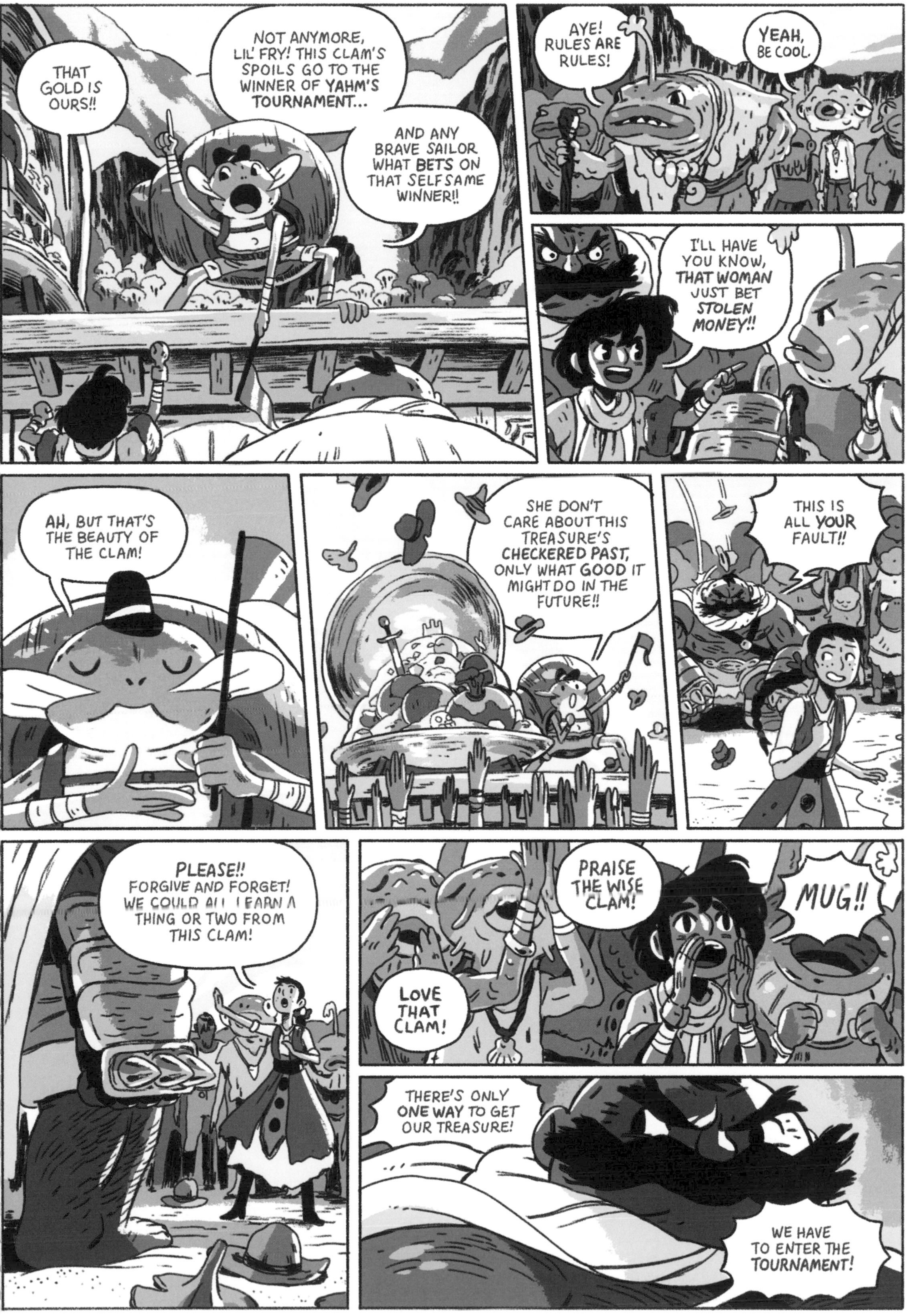
THAT GOLD IS OURS!!
NOT ANYMORE, LIL' FRY! THIS CLAM'S SPOILS GO TO THE WINNER OF YAHM'S TOURNAMENT...
AND ANY BRAVE SAILOR WHAT BETS ON THAT SELFSAME WINNER!!
AYE! RULES ARE RULES!
YEAH, BE COOL.
I'LL HAVE YOU KNOW, THAT WOMAN JUST BET STOLEN MONEY!!
AH, BUT THAT'S THE BEAUTY OF THE CLAM!
SHE DON'T CARE ABOUT THIS TREASURE'S CHECKERED PAST, ONLY WHAT GOOD IT MIGHT DO IN THE FUTURE!!
THIS IS ALL YOUR FAULT!!
PLEASE!! FORGIVE AND FORGET! WE COULD ALL LEARN A THING OR TWO FROM THIS CLAM!
PRAISE THE WISE CLAM!
LOVE THAT CLAM!
MUG!!
THERE'S ONLY ONE WAY TO GET OUR TREASURE!
WE HAVE TO ENTER THE TOURNAMENT!

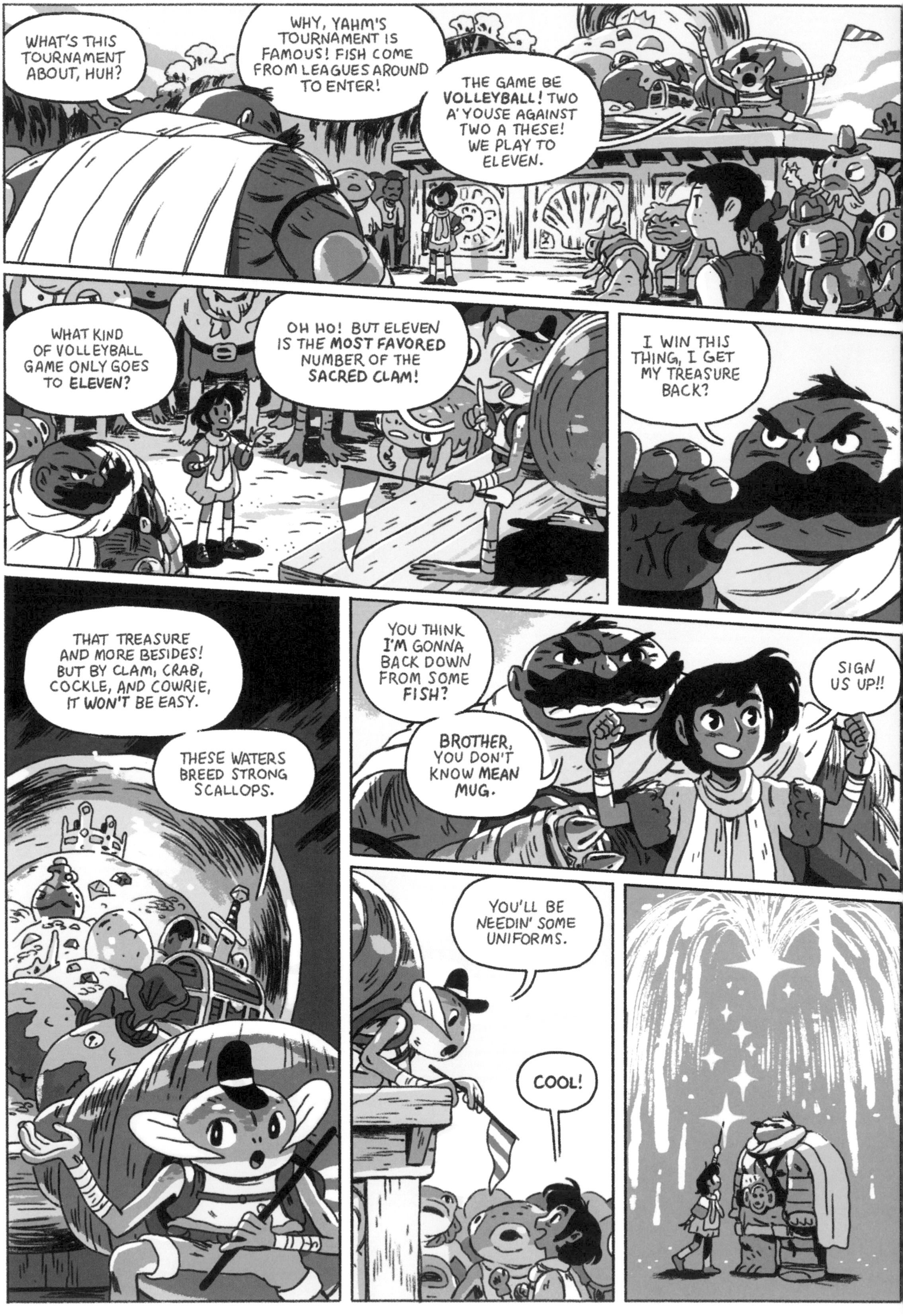
WHAT'S THIS TOURNAMENT ABOUT, HUH?
WHY, YAHM'S TOURNAMENT IS FAMOUS! FISH COME FROM LEAGUES AROUND TO ENTER!
THE GAME BE **VOLLEYBALL!** TWO A' YOUSE AGAINST TWO A THESE! WE PLAY TO ELEVEN.
WHAT KIND OF VOLLEYBALL GAME ONLY GOES TO **ELEVEN?**
OH HO! BUT ELEVEN IS THE **MOST FAVORED** NUMBER OF THE **SACRED CLAM!**
I WIN THIS THING, I GET MY TREASURE BACK?
THAT TREASURE AND MORE BESIDES! BUT BY CLAM, CRAB, COCKLE, AND COWRIE, IT **WON'T** BE EASY.
THESE WATERS BREED STRONG SCALLOPS.
YOU THINK **I'M** GONNA BACK DOWN FROM SOME **FISH?**
BROTHER, YOU DON'T KNOW **MEAN MUG.**
SIGN US UP!!
YOU'LL BE NEEDIN' SOME UNIFORMS.
COOL!

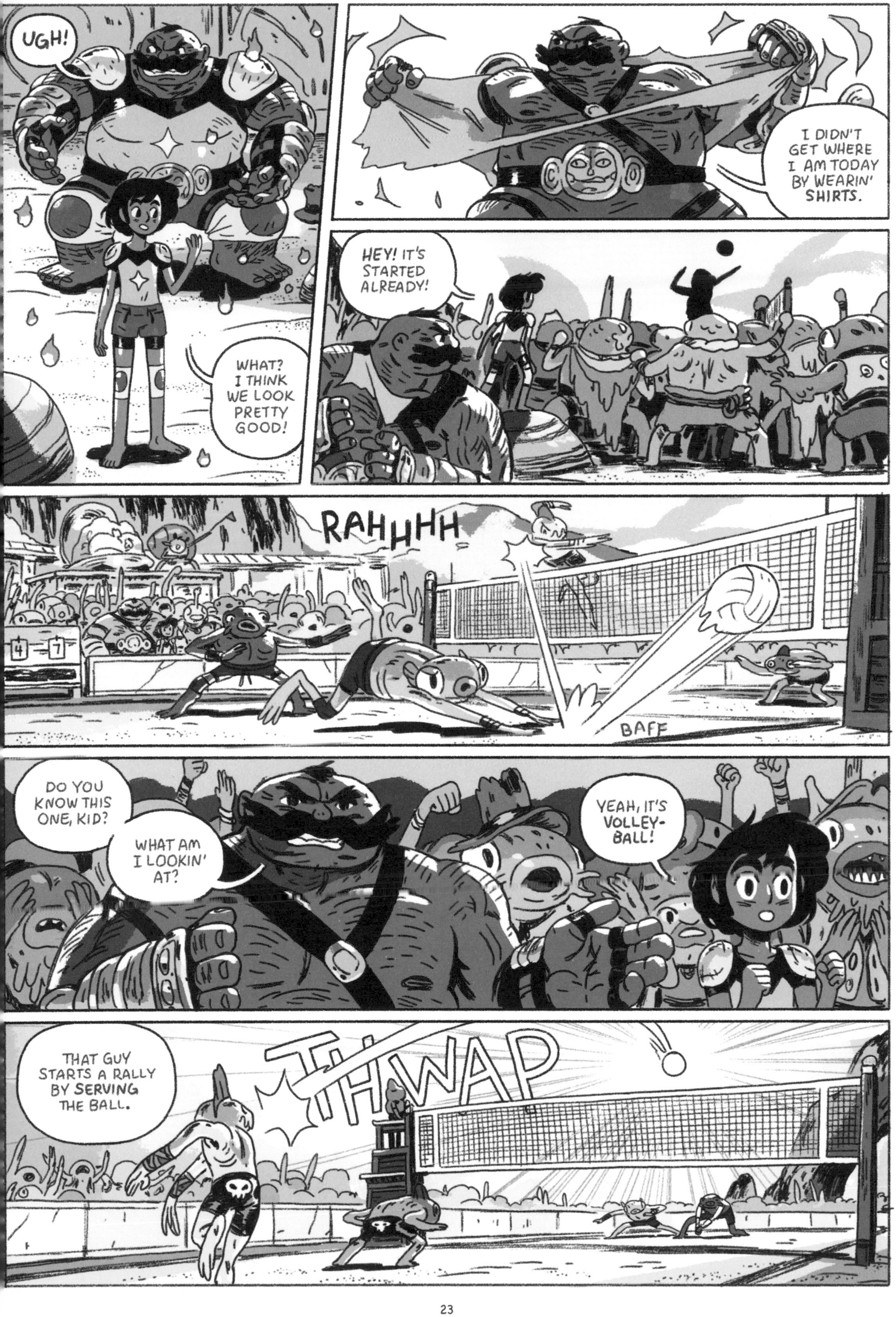

UGH!
WHAT? I THINK WE LOOK PRETTY GOOD!
I DIDN'T GET WHERE I AM TODAY BY WEARIN' SHIRTS.
HEY! IT'S STARTED ALREADY!
RAHHHH
BAFF
DO YOU KNOW THIS ONE, KID?
WHAT AM I LOOKIN' AT?
YEAH, IT'S VOLLEY-BALL!
THAT GUY STARTS A RALLY BY SERVING THE BALL.
THWAP

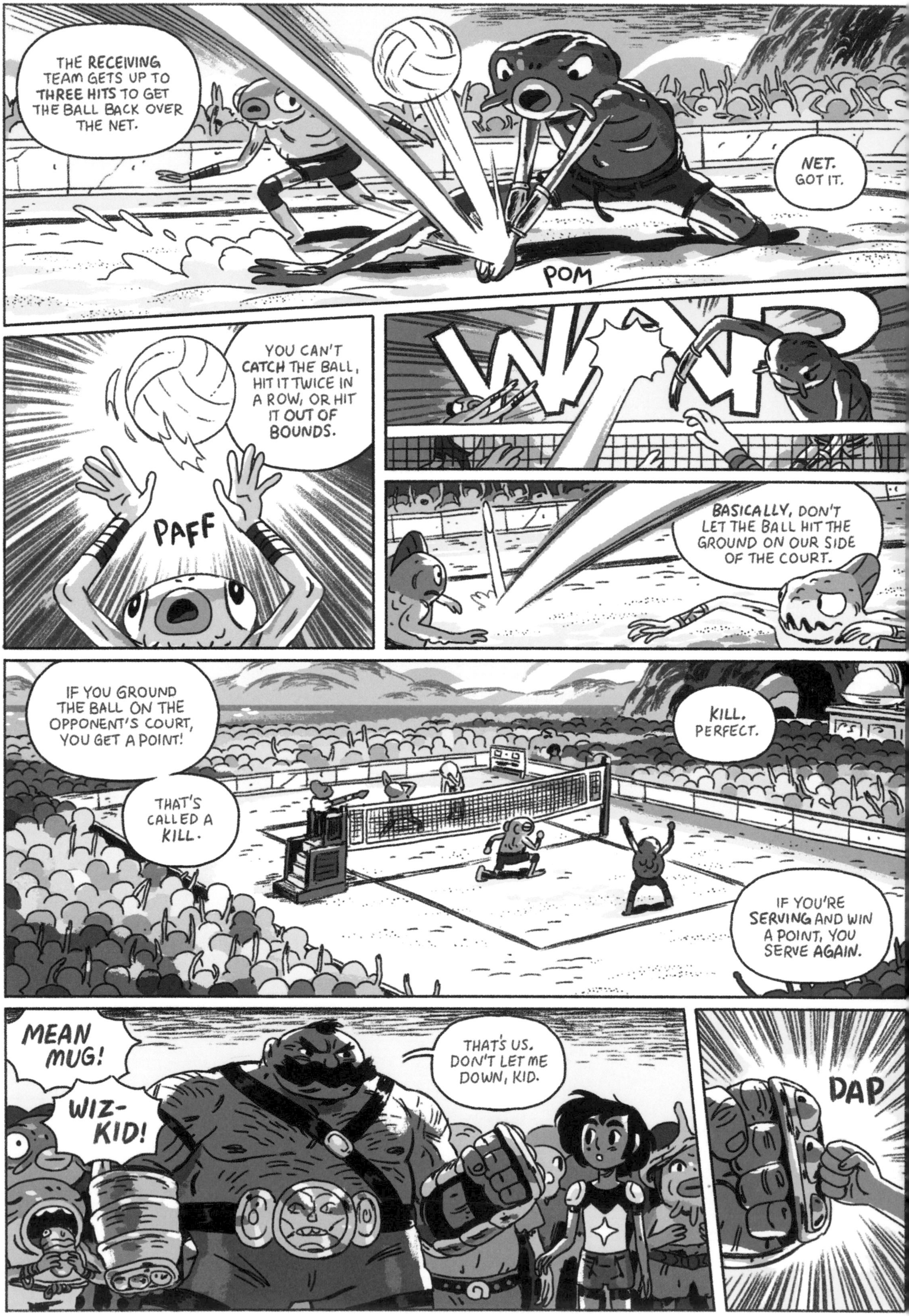
THE RECEIVING TEAM GETS UP TO THREE HITS TO GET THE BALL BACK OVER THE NET.
NET. GOT IT.
POM
YOU CAN'T CATCH THE BALL, HIT IT TWICE IN A ROW, OR HIT IT OUT OF BOUNDS.
PAFF
BASICALLY, DON'T LET THE BALL HIT THE GROUND ON OUR SIDE OF THE COURT.
IF YOU GROUND THE BALL ON THE OPPONENT'S COURT, YOU GET A POINT!
THAT'S CALLED A KILL.
KILL. PERFECT.
IF YOU'RE SERVING AND WIN A POINT, YOU SERVE AGAIN.
MEAN MUG!
WIZ-KID!
THAT'S US. DON'T LET ME DOWN, KID.
DAP

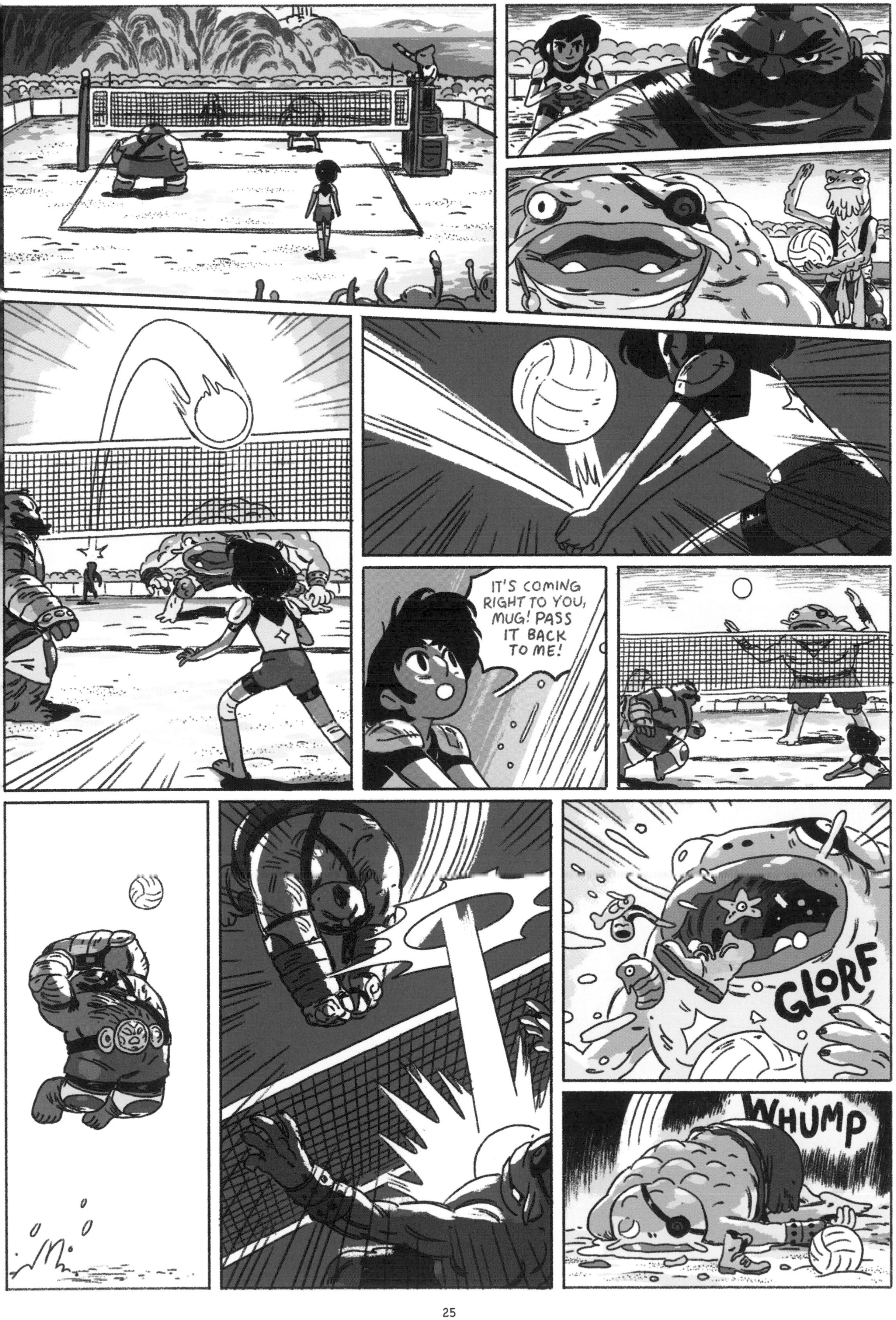

IT'S COMING RIGHT TO YOU, MUG! PASS IT BACK TO ME!
GLORF
WHUMP

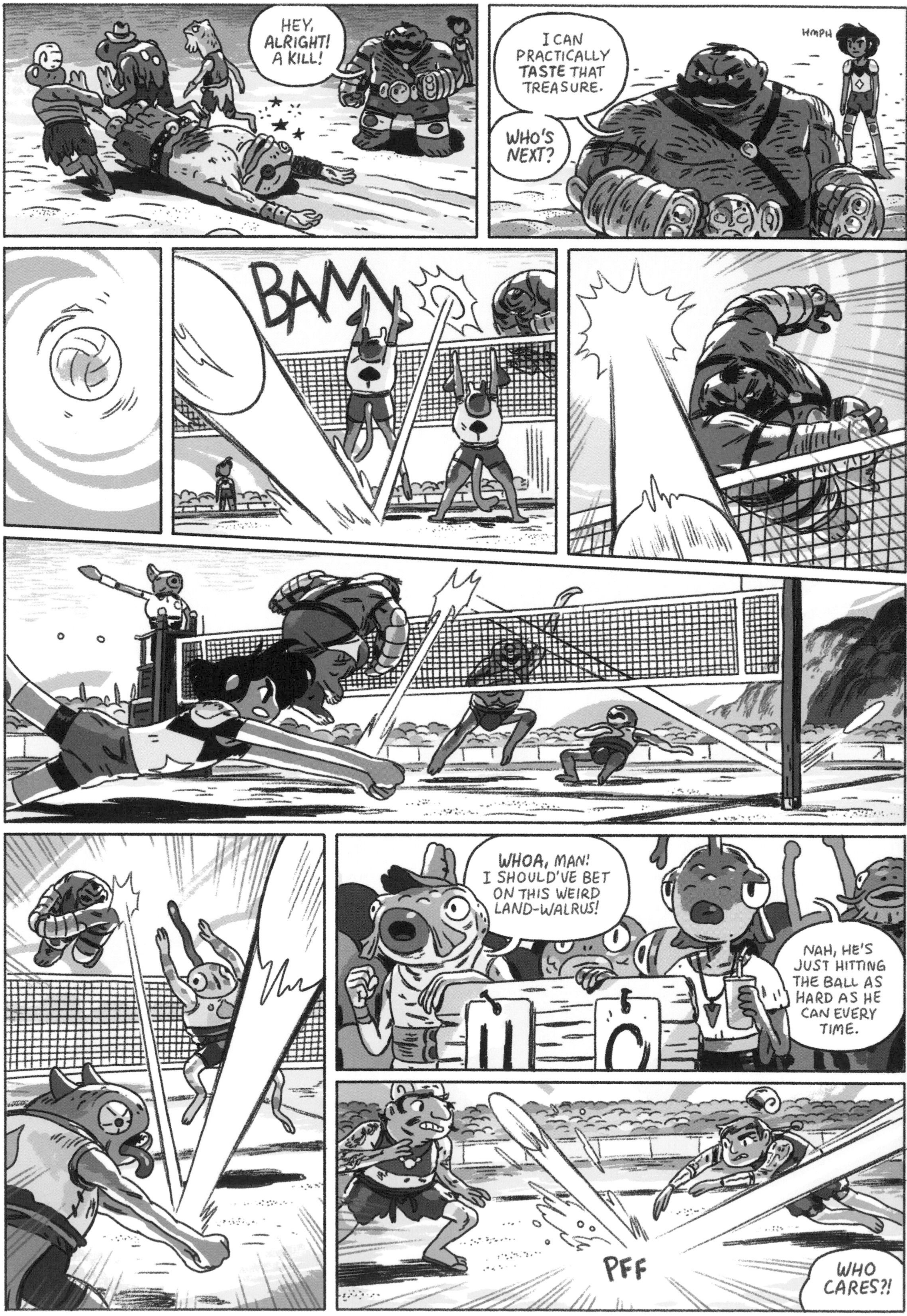
HEY, ALRIGHT! A KILL!
I CAN PRACTICALLY TASTE THAT TREASURE.
WHO'S NEXT?
HMPH
BAM
WHOA, MAN! I SHOULD'VE BET ON THIS WEIRD LAND-WALRUS!
NAH, HE'S JUST HITTING THE BALL AS HARD AS HE CAN EVERY TIME.
PFF
WHO CARES?!

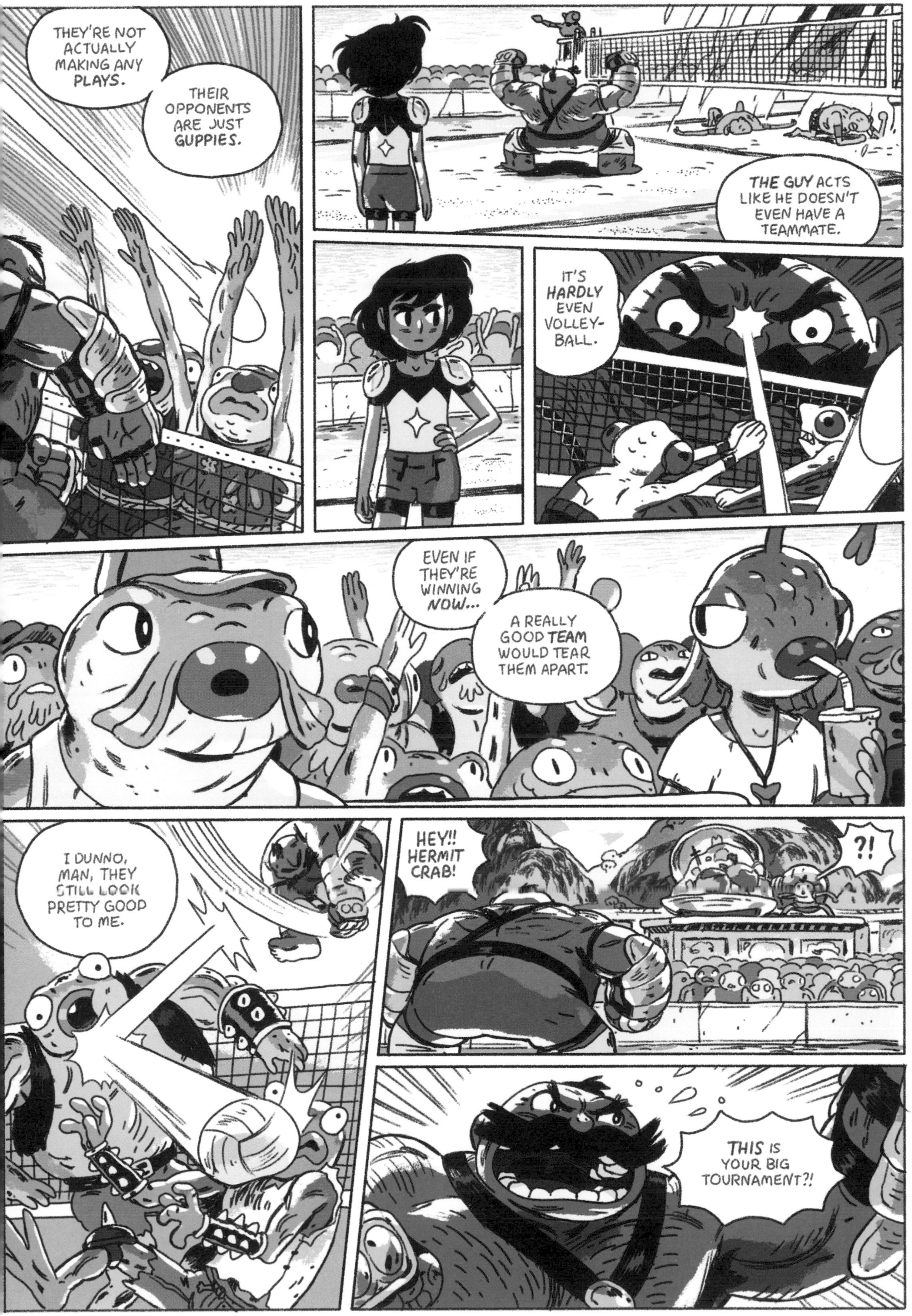

THEY'RE NOT ACTUALLY MAKING ANY PLAYS.
THEIR OPPONENTS ARE JUST GUPPIES.
THE GUY ACTS LIKE HE DOESN'T EVEN HAVE A TEAMMATE.
IT'S HARDLY EVEN VOLLEY-BALL.
EVEN IF THEY'RE WINNING NOW...
A REALLY GOOD TEAM WOULD TEAR THEM APART.
I DUNNO, MAN, THEY STILL LOOK PRETTY GOOD TO ME.
HEY!! HERMIT CRAB!
?!
THIS IS YOUR BIG TOURNAMENT?!

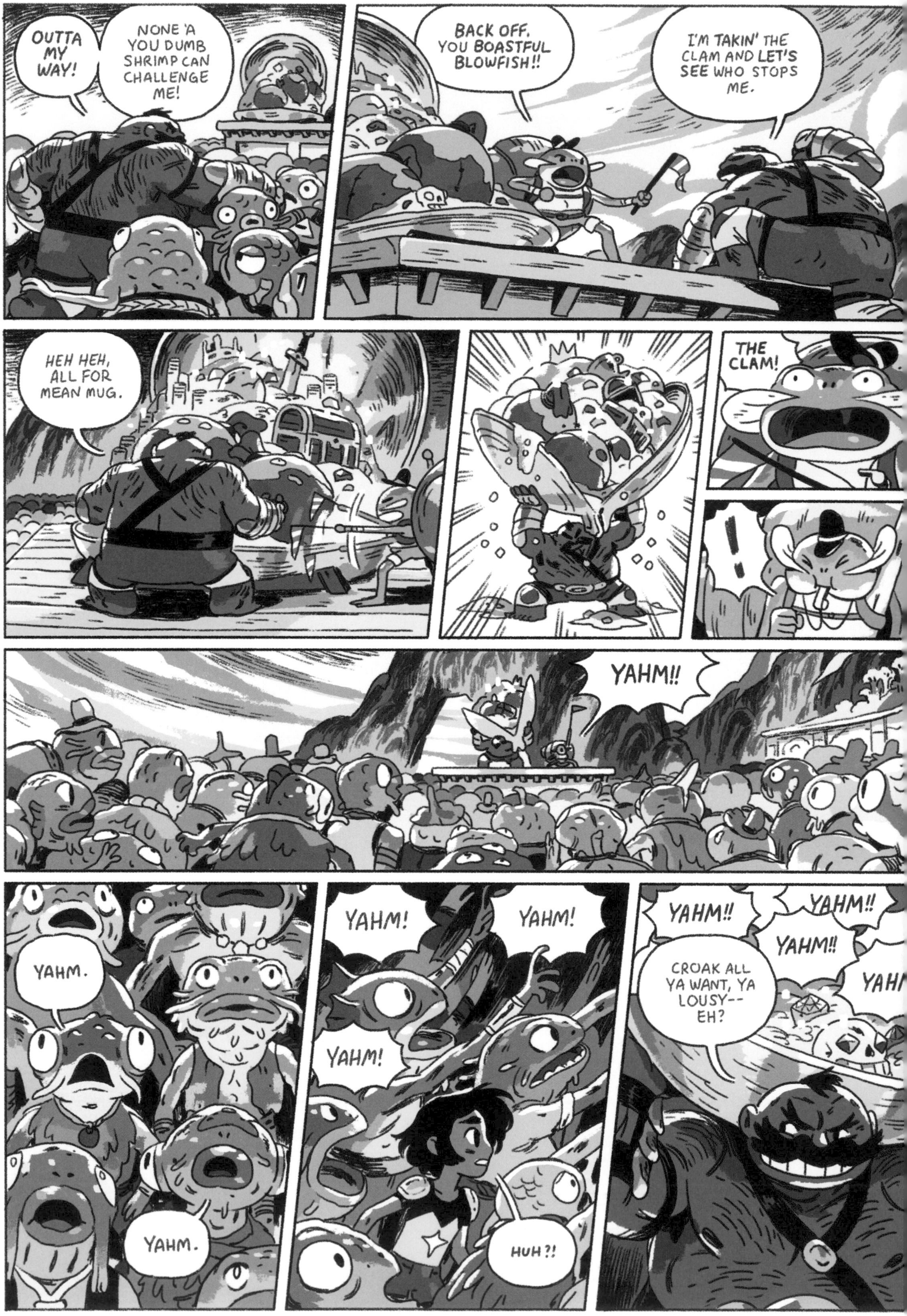
OUTTA MY WAY!
NONE 'A YOU DUMB SHRIMP CAN CHALLENGE ME!
BACK OFF, YOU BOASTFUL BLOWFISH!!
I'M TAKIN' THE CLAM AND LET'S SEE WHO STOPS ME.
HEH HEH, ALL FOR MEAN MUG.
THE CLAM!
!
YAHM!!
YAHM.
YAHM.
YAHM!
YAHM!
YAHM!
HUH?!
YAHM!!
YAHM!!
YAHM!!
CROAK ALL YA WANT, YA LOUSY-- EH?

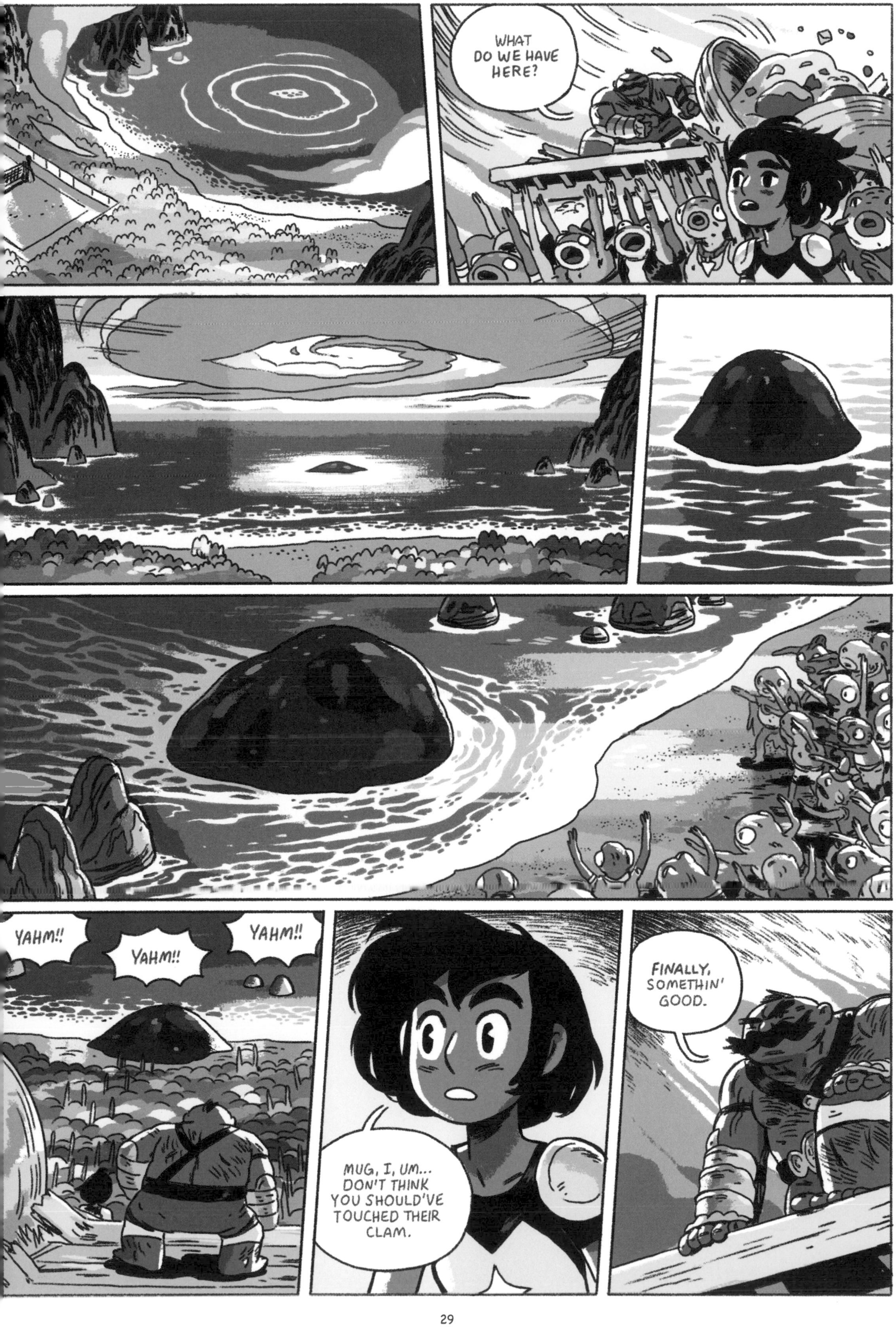
WHAT DO WE HAVE HERE?
YAHM!!
YAHM!!
YAHM!!
MUG, I, UM... DON'T THINK YOU SHOULD'VE TOUCHED THEIR CLAM.
FINALLY, SOMETHIN' GOOD.

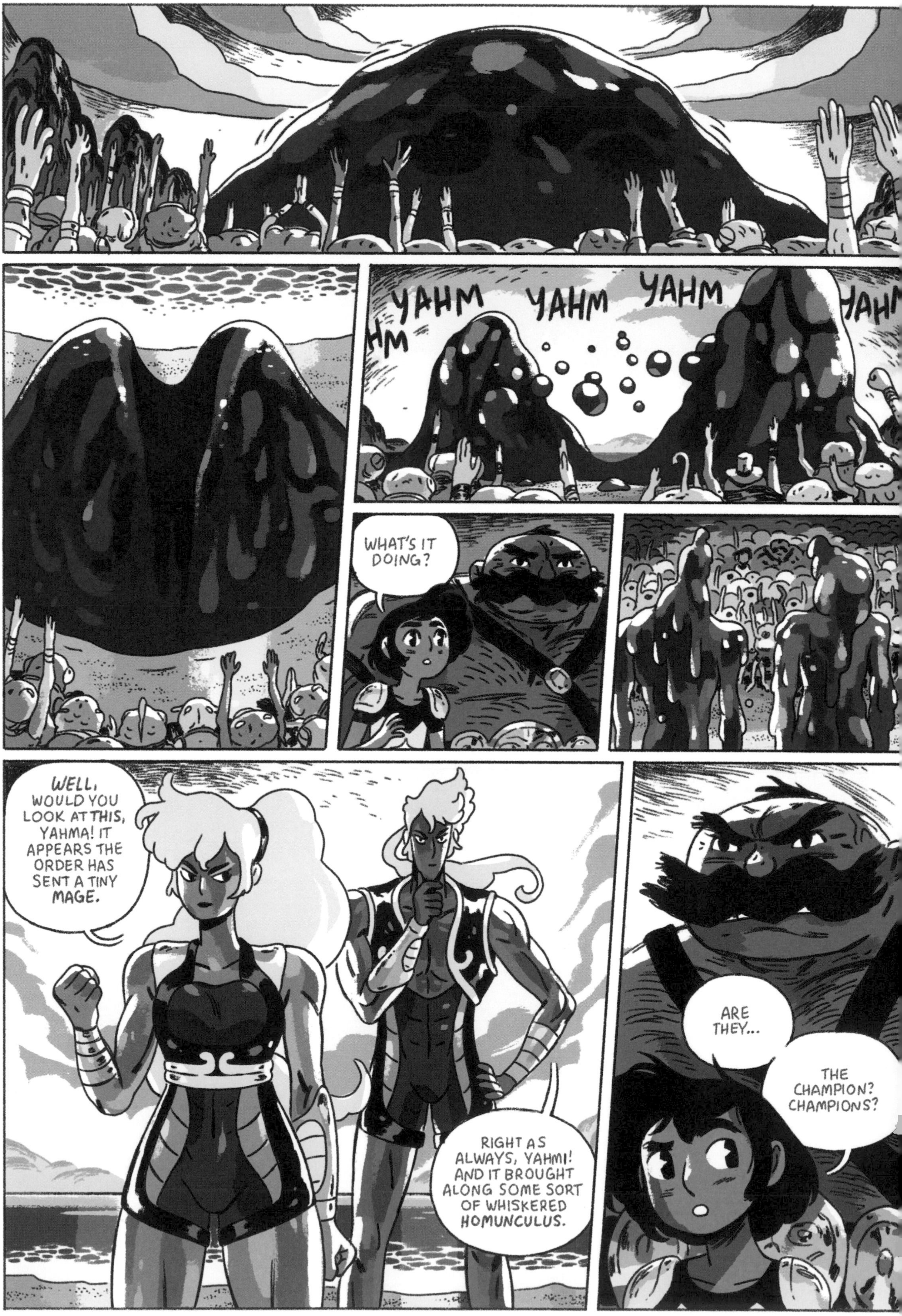
YAHM
YAHM
YAHM
YAHM
HM
WHAT'S IT DOING?
WELL, WOULD YOU LOOK AT THIS, YAHMA! IT APPEARS THE ORDER HAS SENT A TINY MAGE.
RIGHT AS ALWAYS, YAHMI! AND IT BROUGHT ALONG SOME SORT OF WHISKERED HOMUNCULUS.
ARE THEY...
THE CHAMPION? CHAMPIONS?

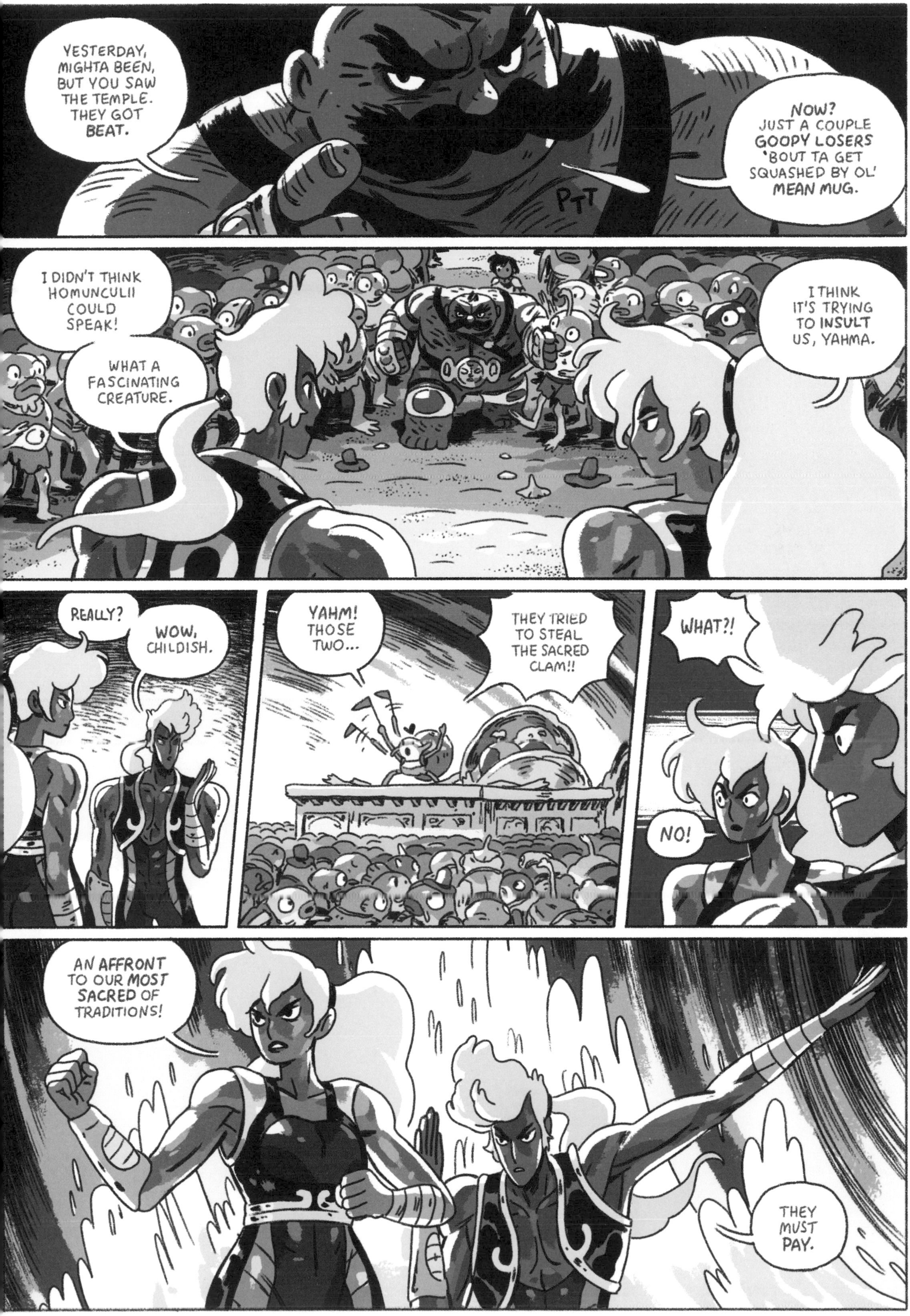

YESTERDAY, MIGHTA BEEN, BUT YOU SAW THE TEMPLE. THEY GOT BEAT.
NOW? JUST A COUPLE GOOPY LOSERS 'BOUT TA GET SQUASHED BY OL' MEAN MUG.
PTT
I DIDN'T THINK HOMUNCULII COULD SPEAK!
WHAT A FASCINATING CREATURE.
I THINK IT'S TRYING TO INSULT US, YAHMA.
REALLY?
WOW, CHILDISH.
YAHM! THOSE TWO...
THEY TRIED TO STEAL THE SACRED CLAM!!
WHAT?!
NO!
AN AFFRONT TO OUR MOST SACRED OF TRADITIONS!
THEY MUST PAY.

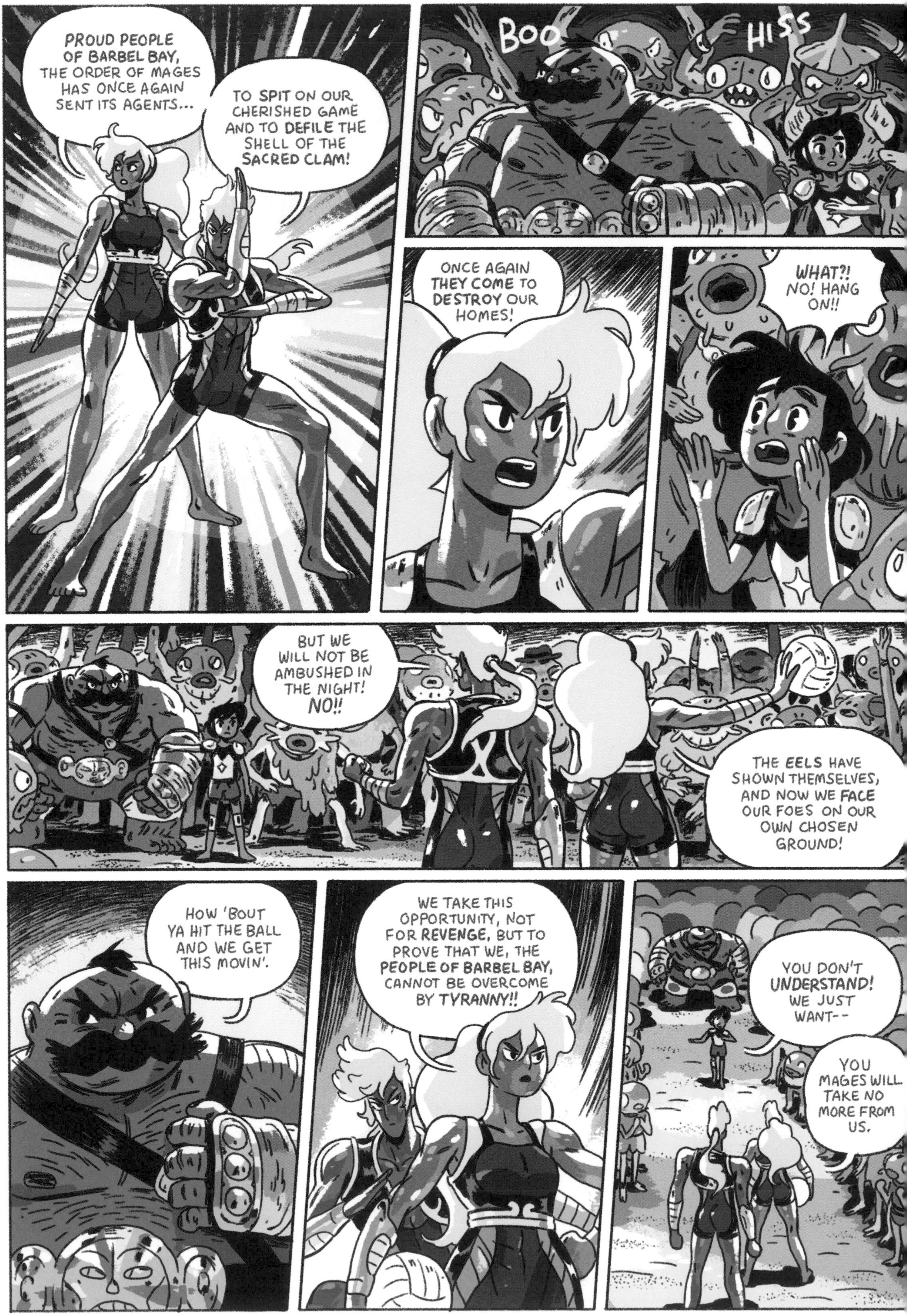
BOO
HISS
PROUD PEOPLE OF BARBEL BAY, THE ORDER OF MAGES HAS ONCE AGAIN SENT ITS AGENTS...
TO SPIT ON OUR CHERISHED GAME AND TO DEFILE THE SHELL OF THE SACRED CLAM!
ONCE AGAIN THEY COME TO DESTROY OUR HOMES!
WHAT?! NO! HANG ON!!
BUT WE WILL NOT BE AMBUSHED IN THE NIGHT! NO!!
THE EELS HAVE SHOWN THEMSELVES, AND NOW WE FACE OUR FOES ON OUR OWN CHOSEN GROUND!
HOW 'BOUT YA HIT THE BALL AND WE GET THIS MOVIN'.
WE TAKE THIS OPPORTUNITY, NOT FOR REVENGE, BUT TO PROVE THAT WE, THE PEOPLE OF BARBEL BAY, CANNOT BE OVERCOME BY TYRANNY!!
YOU DON'T UNDERSTAND! WE JUST WANT--
YOU MAGES WILL TAKE NO MORE FROM US.

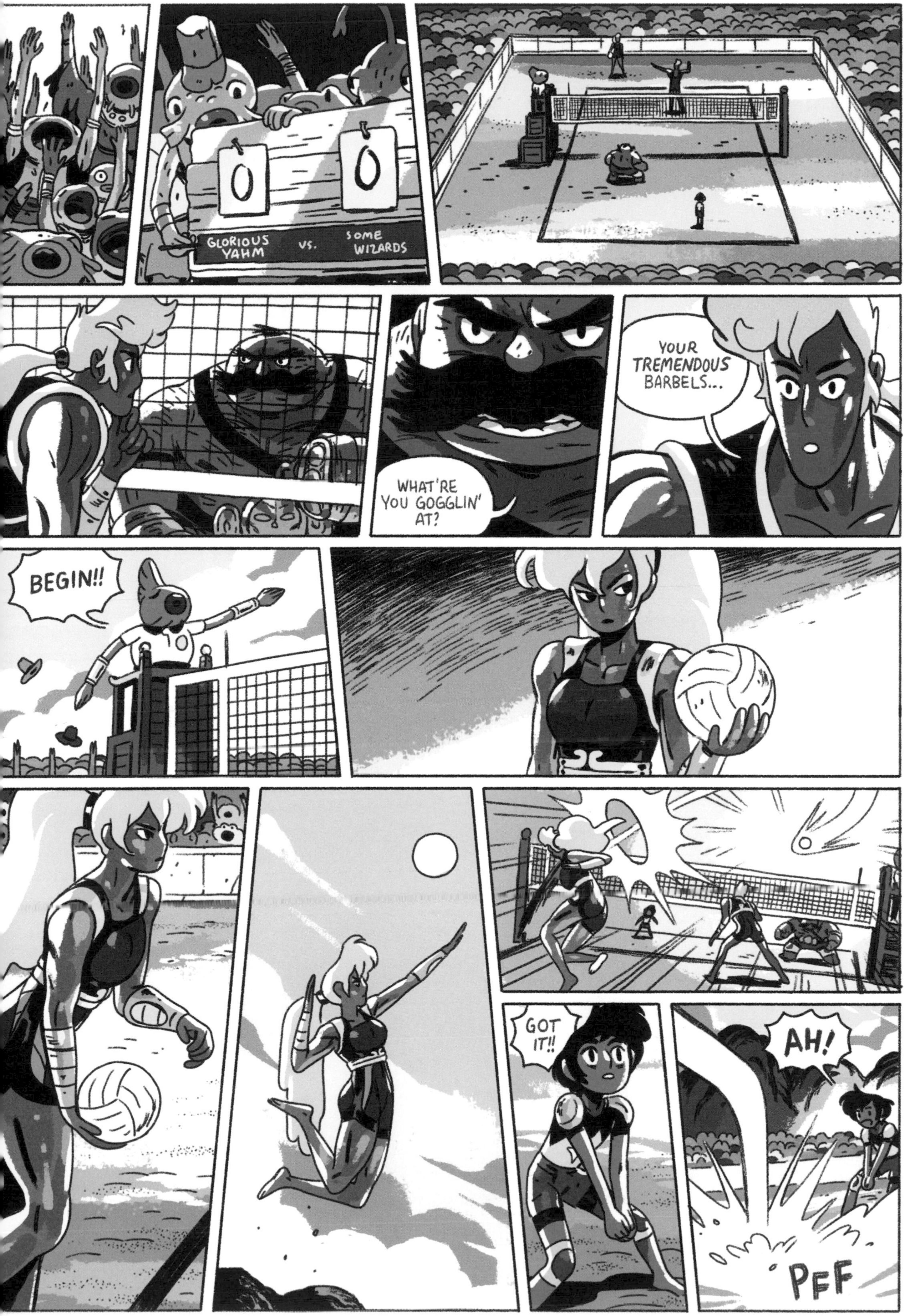
0
0
GLORIOUS YAHM
VS.
SOME WIZARDS
YOUR TREMENDOUS BARBELS...
WHAT'RE YOU GOGGLIN' AT?
BEGIN!!
GOT IT!!
AH!
PFF

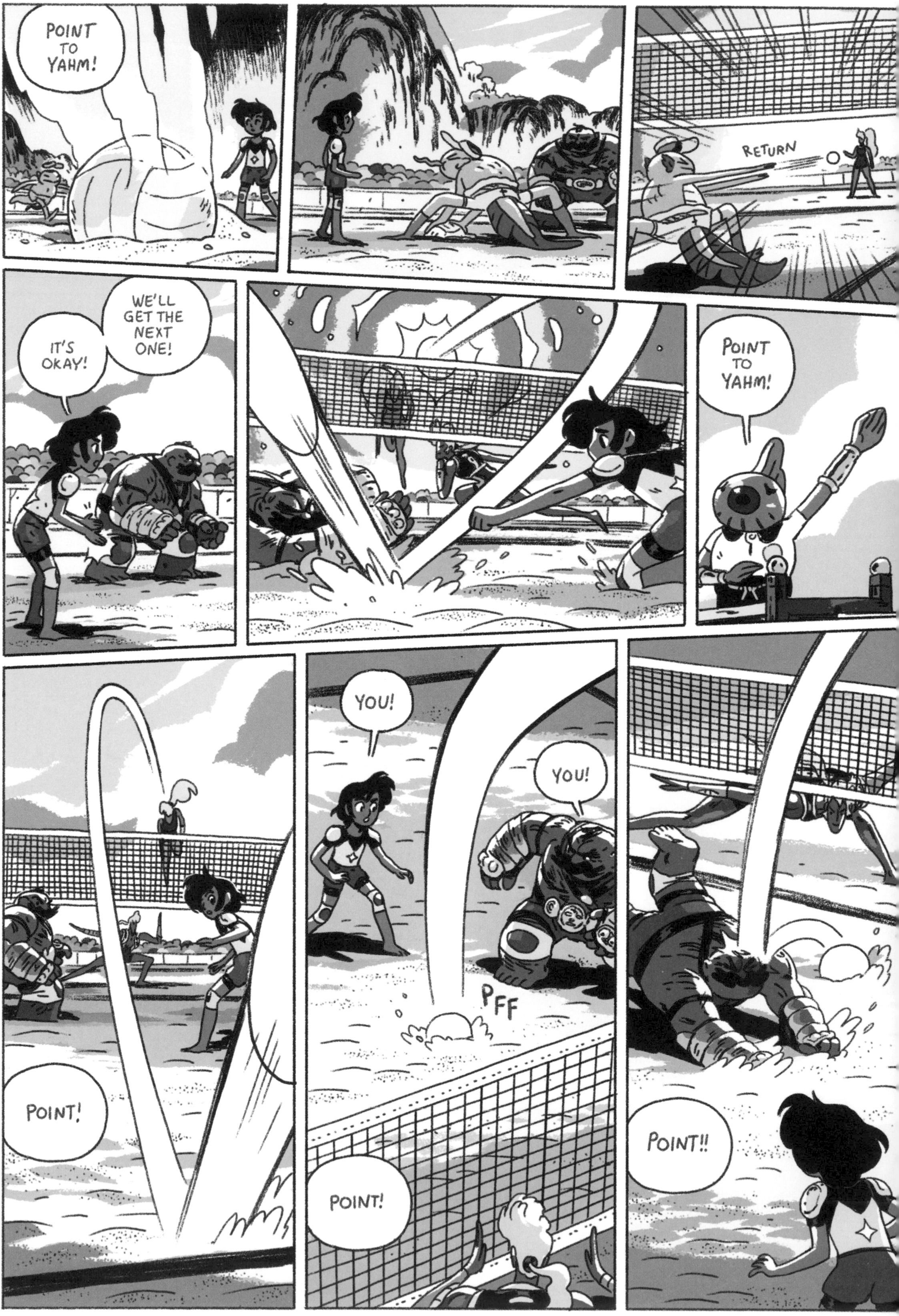
POINT TO YAHM!
RETURN
IT'S OKAY!
WE'LL GET THE NEXT ONE!
POINT TO YAHM!
POINT!
YOU!
YOU!
PFF
POINT!
POINT!!

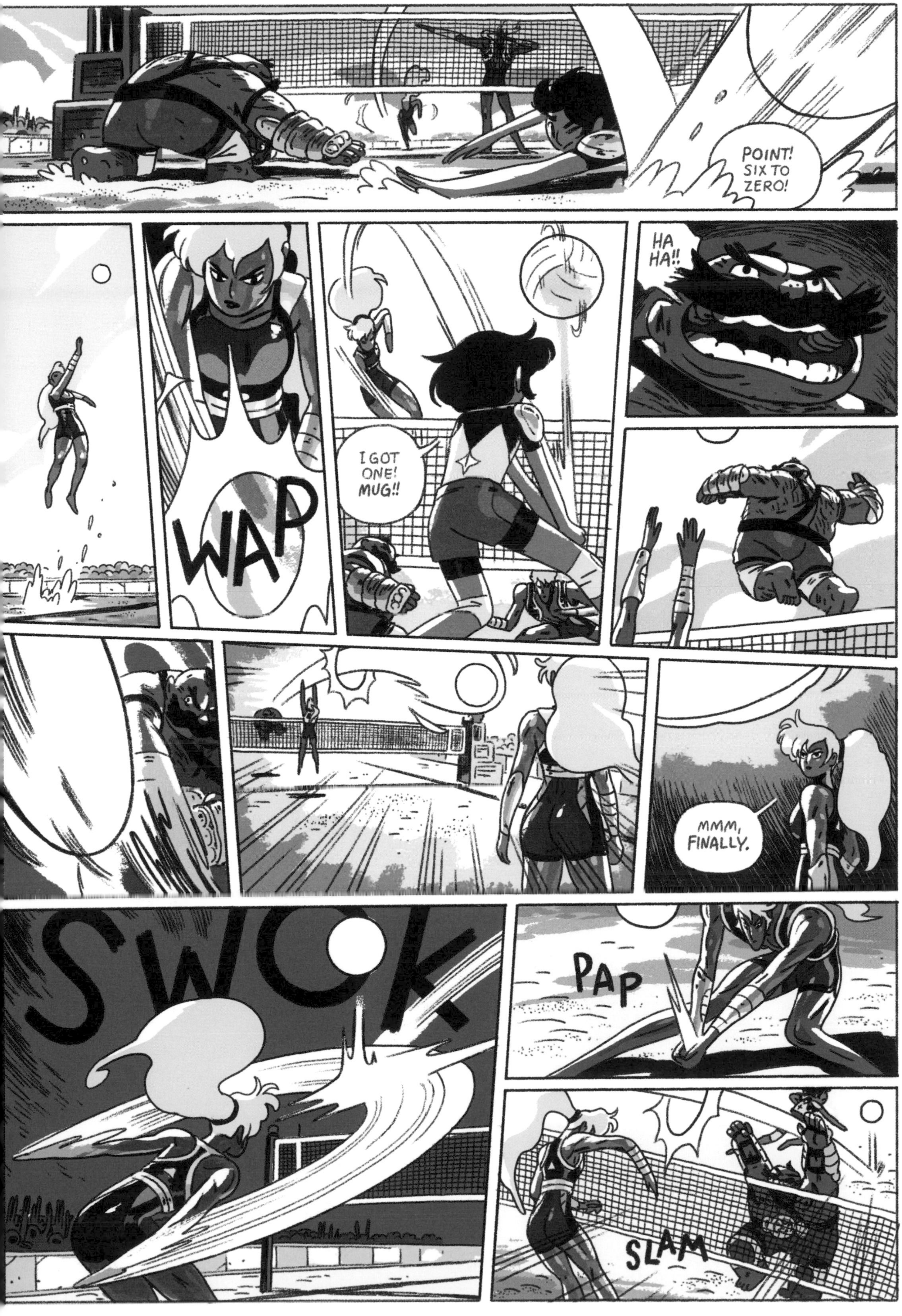
POINT! SIX TO ZERO!
WAP
I GOT ONE! MUG!!
HA HA!!
MMM, FINALLY.
SWOCK
PAP
SLAM

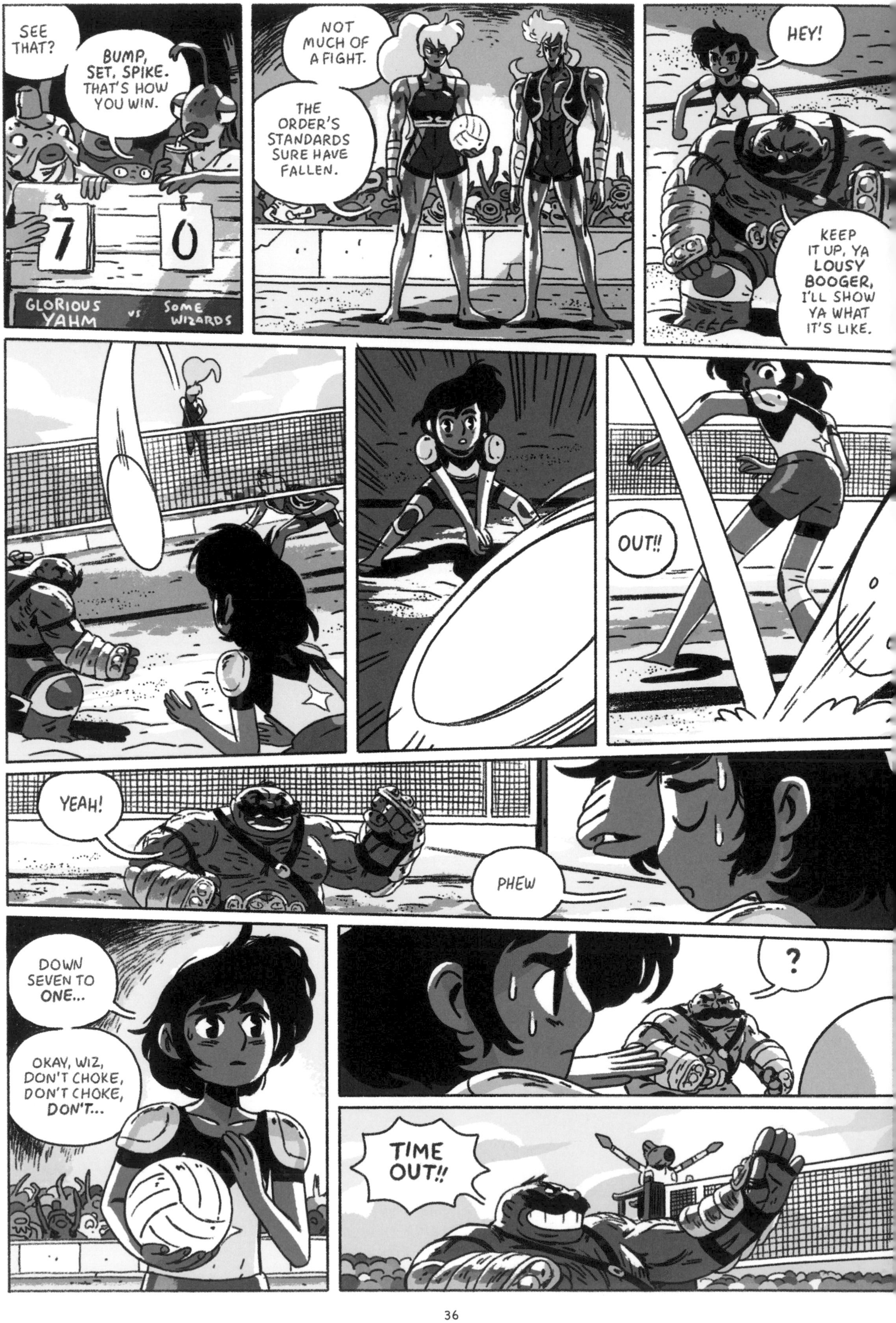
SEE THAT?
BUMP, SET, SPIKE. THAT'S HOW YOU WIN.
7
0
GLORIOUS YAHM vs SOME WIZARDS
NOT MUCH OF A FIGHT.
THE ORDER'S STANDARDS SURE HAVE FALLEN.
HEY!
KEEP IT UP, YA LOUSY BOOGER, I'LL SHOW YA WHAT IT'S LIKE.
OUT!!
YEAH!
PHEW
DOWN SEVEN TO ONE...
OKAY, WIZ, DON'T CHOKE, DON'T CHOKE, DON'T...
?
TIME OUT!!

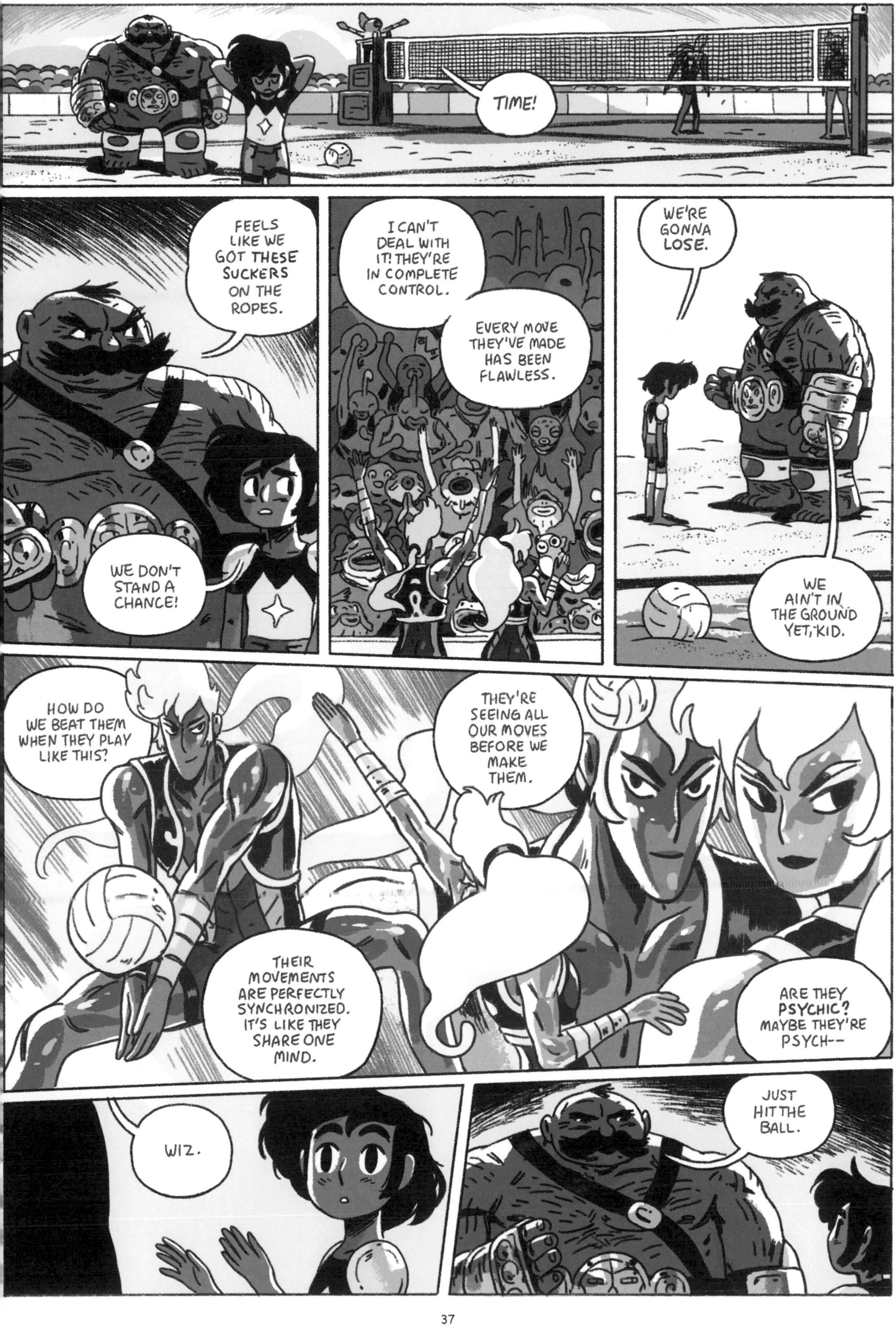

TIME!
FEELS LIKE WE GOT THESE SUCKERS ON THE ROPES.
WE DON'T STAND A CHANCE!
I CAN'T DEAL WITH IT! THEY'RE IN COMPLETE CONTROL.
EVERY MOVE THEY'VE MADE HAS BEEN FLAWLESS.
WE'RE GONNA LOSE.
WE AIN'T IN THE GROUND YET, KID.
HOW DO WE BEAT THEM WHEN THEY PLAY LIKE THIS?
THEY'RE SEEING ALL OUR MOVES BEFORE WE MAKE THEM.
THEIR MOVEMENTS ARE PERFECTLY SYNCHRONIZED. IT'S LIKE THEY SHARE ONE MIND.
ARE THEY PSYCHIC? MAYBE THEY'RE PSYCH--
WIZ.
JUST HIT THE BALL.

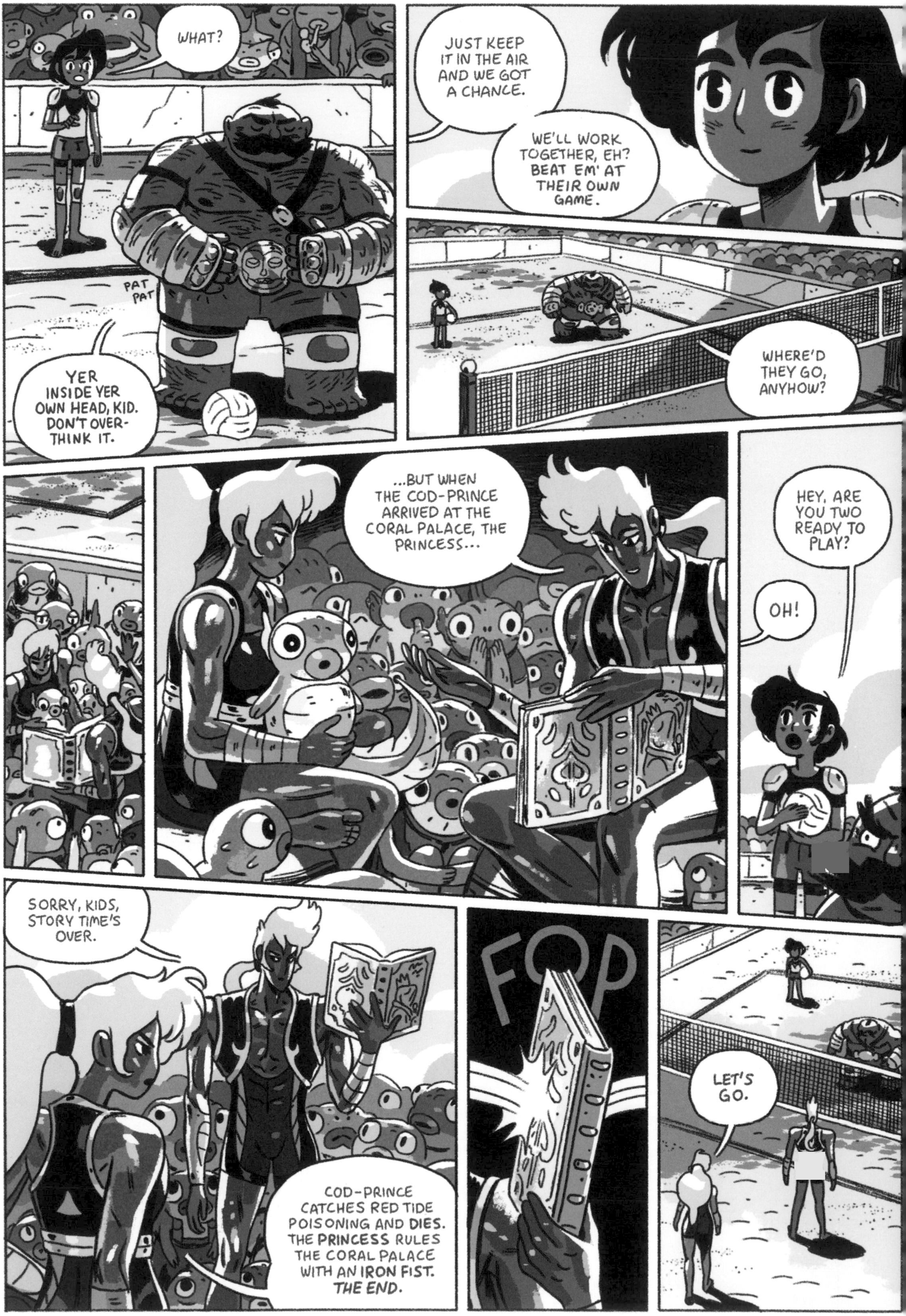
WHAT?
PAT PAT
YER INSIDE YER OWN HEAD, KID. DON'T OVER-THINK IT.
JUST KEEP IT IN THE AIR AND WE GOT A CHANCE.
WE'LL WORK TOGETHER, EH? BEAT EM' AT THEIR OWN GAME.
WHERE'D THEY GO, ANYHOW?
...BUT WHEN THE COD-PRINCE ARRIVED AT THE CORAL PALACE, THE PRINCESS...
HEY, ARE YOU TWO READY TO PLAY?
OH!
SORRY, KIDS, STORY TIME'S OVER.
COD-PRINCE CATCHES RED TIDE POISONING AND DIES. THE PRINCESS RULES THE CORAL PALACE WITH AN IRON FIST. THE END.
FOP
LET'S GO.

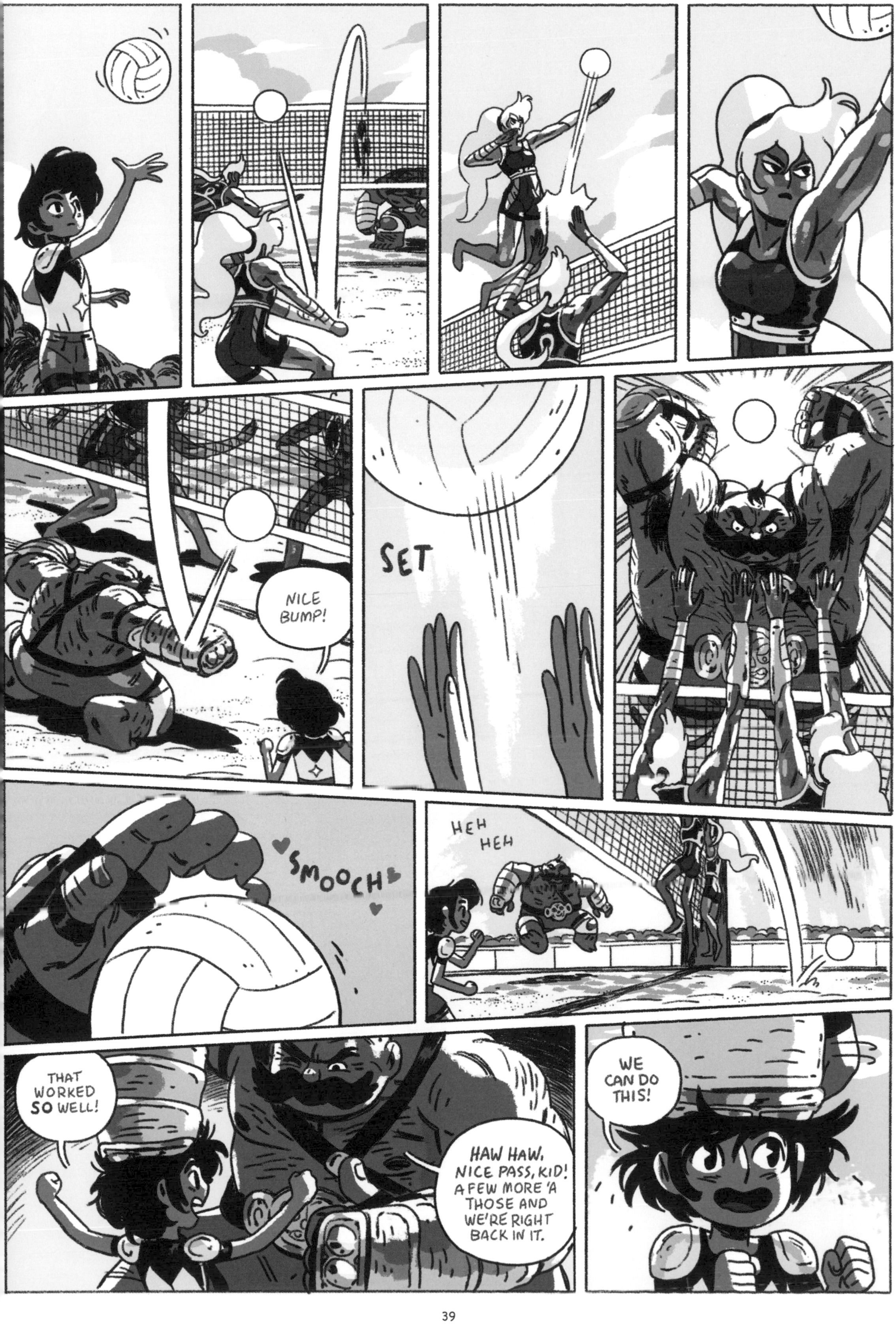
NICE BUMP!
SET
SMOOCH
HEH HEH
THAT WORKED SO WELL!
HAW HAW. NICE PASS, KID! A FEW MORE 'A THOSE AND WE'RE RIGHT BACK IN IT.
WE CAN DO THIS!

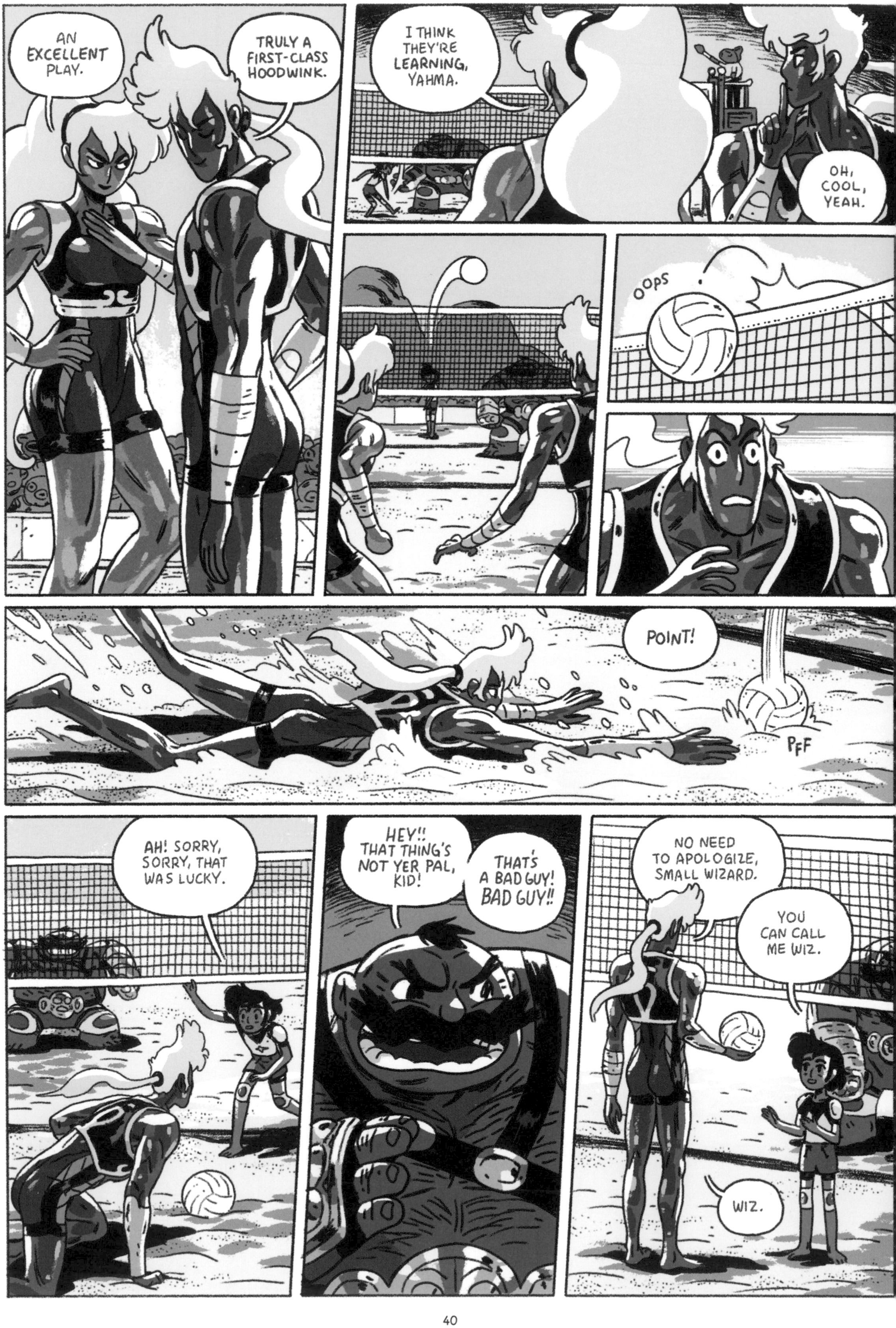
AN EXCELLENT PLAY.
TRULY A FIRST-CLASS HOODWINK.
I THINK THEY'RE LEARNING, YAHMA.
OH, COOL, YEAH.
OOPS
POINT!
PFF
AH! SORRY, SORRY, THAT WAS LUCKY.
HEY!! THAT THING'S NOT YER PAL, KID!
THAT'S A BAD GUY! BAD GUY!!
NO NEED TO APOLOGIZE, SMALL WIZARD.
YOU CAN CALL ME WIZ.
WIZ.

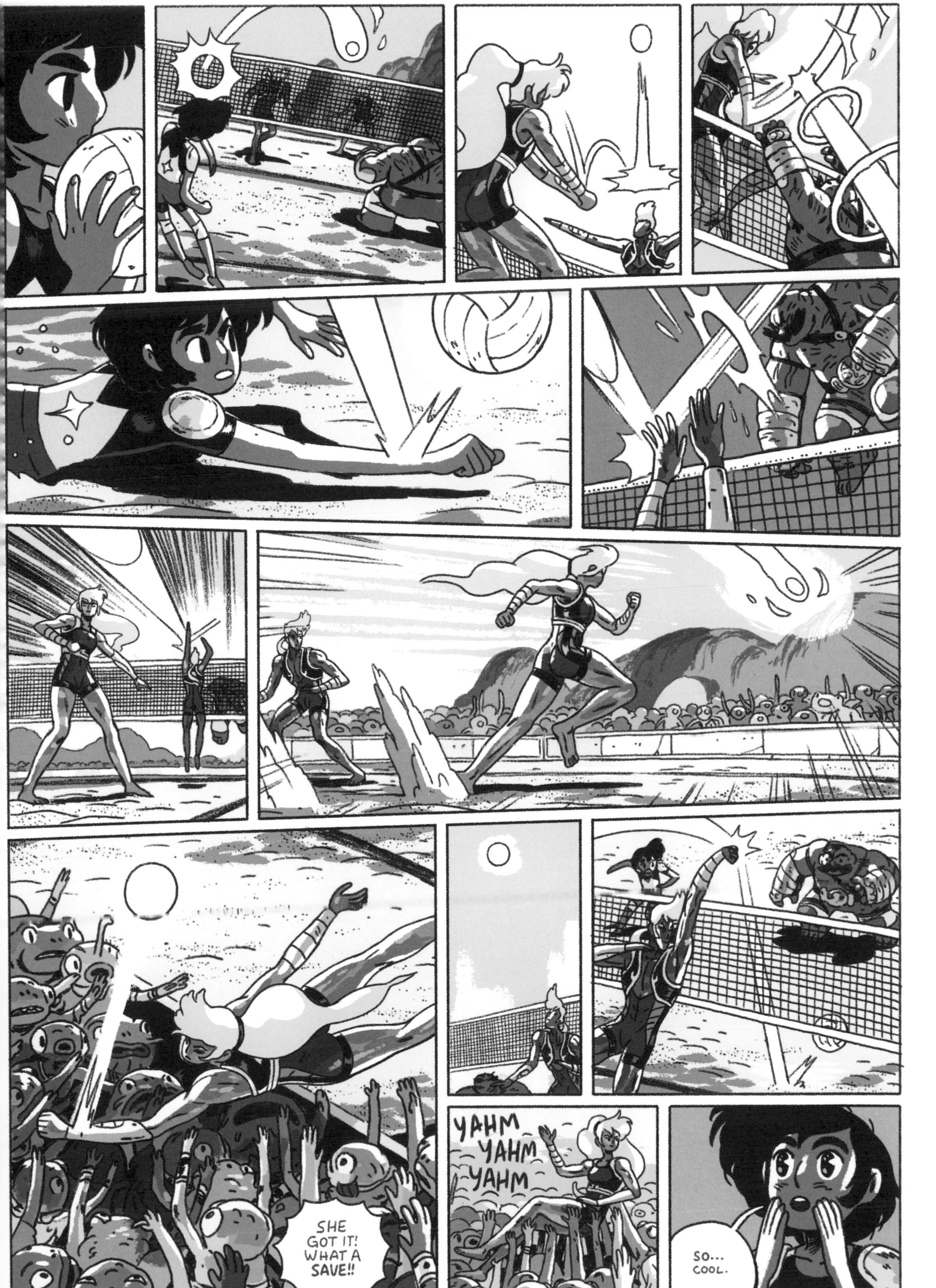
SHE GOT IT! WHAT A SAVE!!
YAHM YAHM YAHM
SO... COOL.

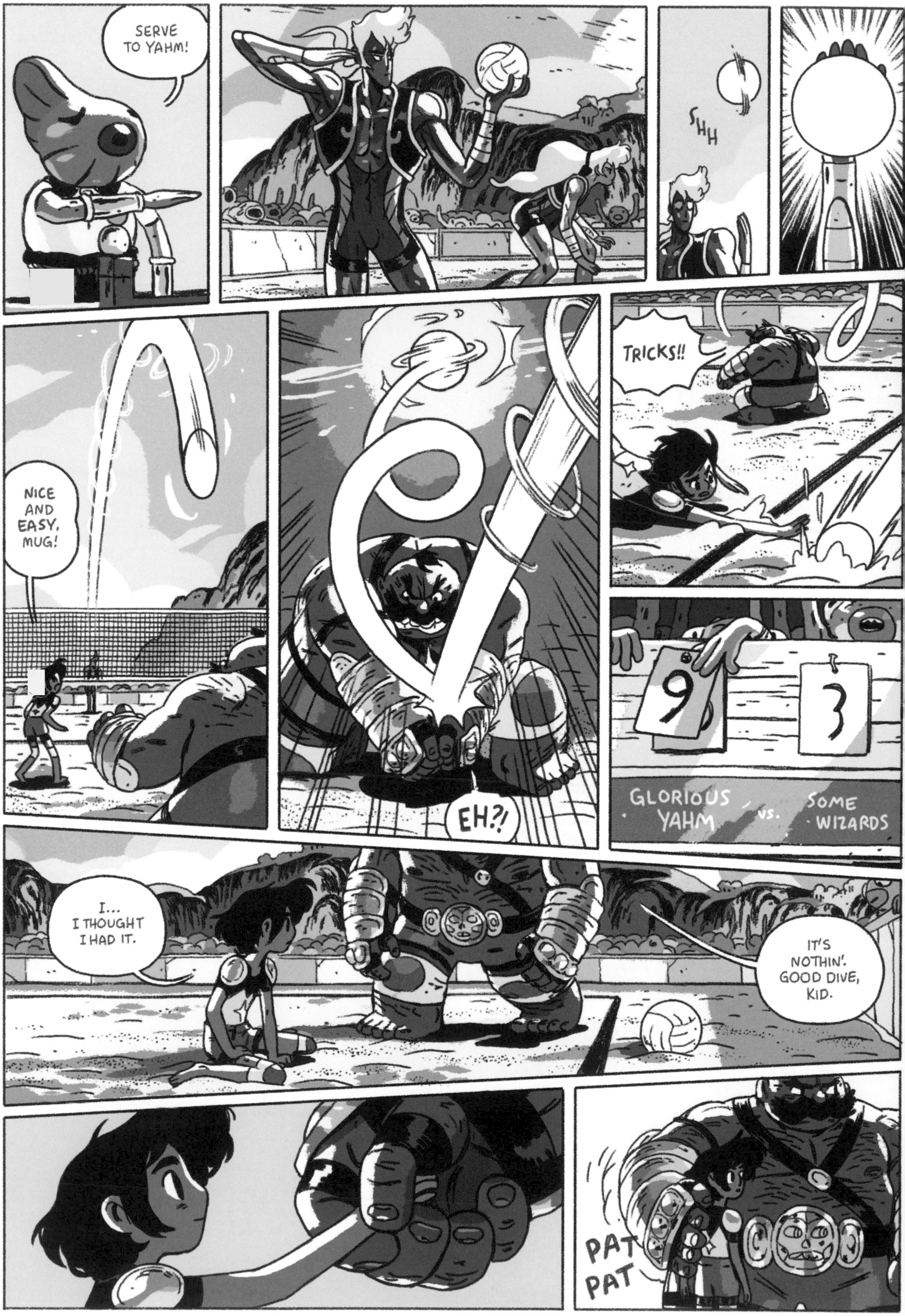

SERVE TO YAHM!
SHH
NICE AND EASY, MUG!
TRICKS!!
EH?!
9
3
GLORIOUS YAHM vs. SOME WIZARDS
I... I THOUGHT I HAD IT.
IT'S NOTHIN'. GOOD DIVE, KID.
PAT PAT

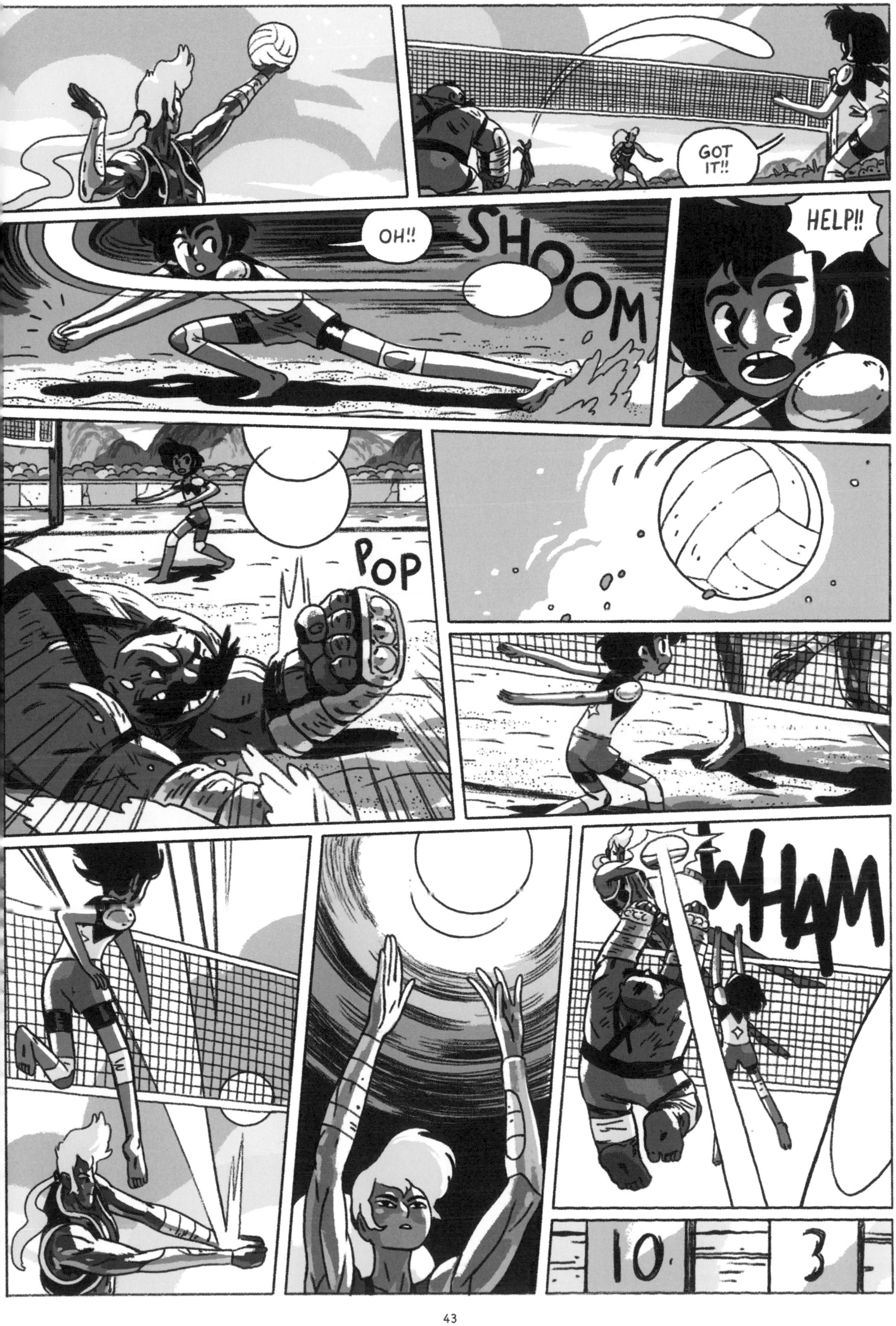
GOT IT!!
OH!!
SHOOM
HELP!!
POP
WHAM
10
3

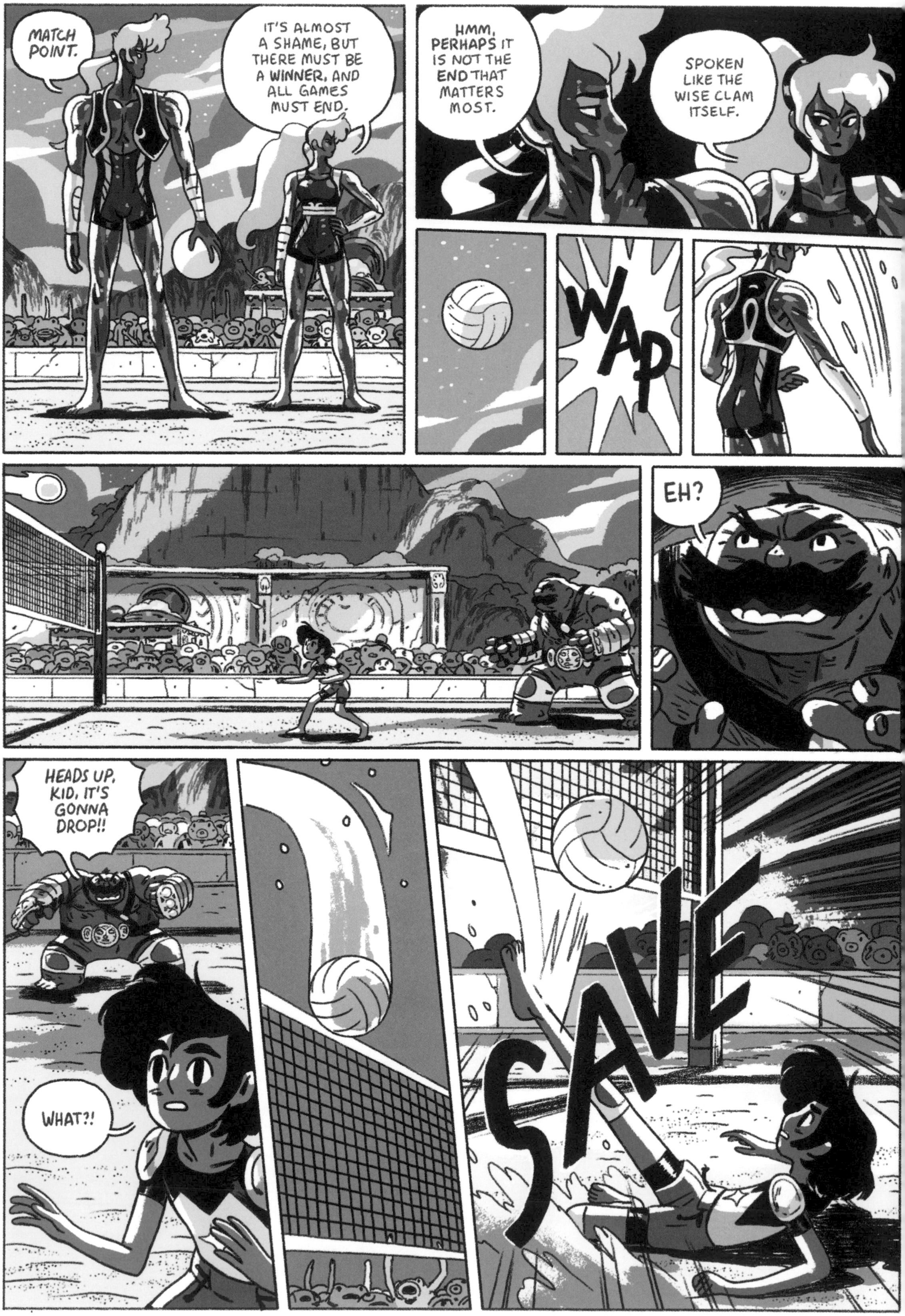
MATCH POINT.
IT'S ALMOST A SHAME, BUT THERE MUST BE A WINNER, AND ALL GAMES MUST END.
HMM, PERHAPS IT IS NOT THE END THAT MATTERS MOST.
SPOKEN LIKE THE WISE CLAM ITSELF.
WAP
EH?
HEADS UP, KID, IT'S GONNA DROP!!
WHAT?!
SAVE

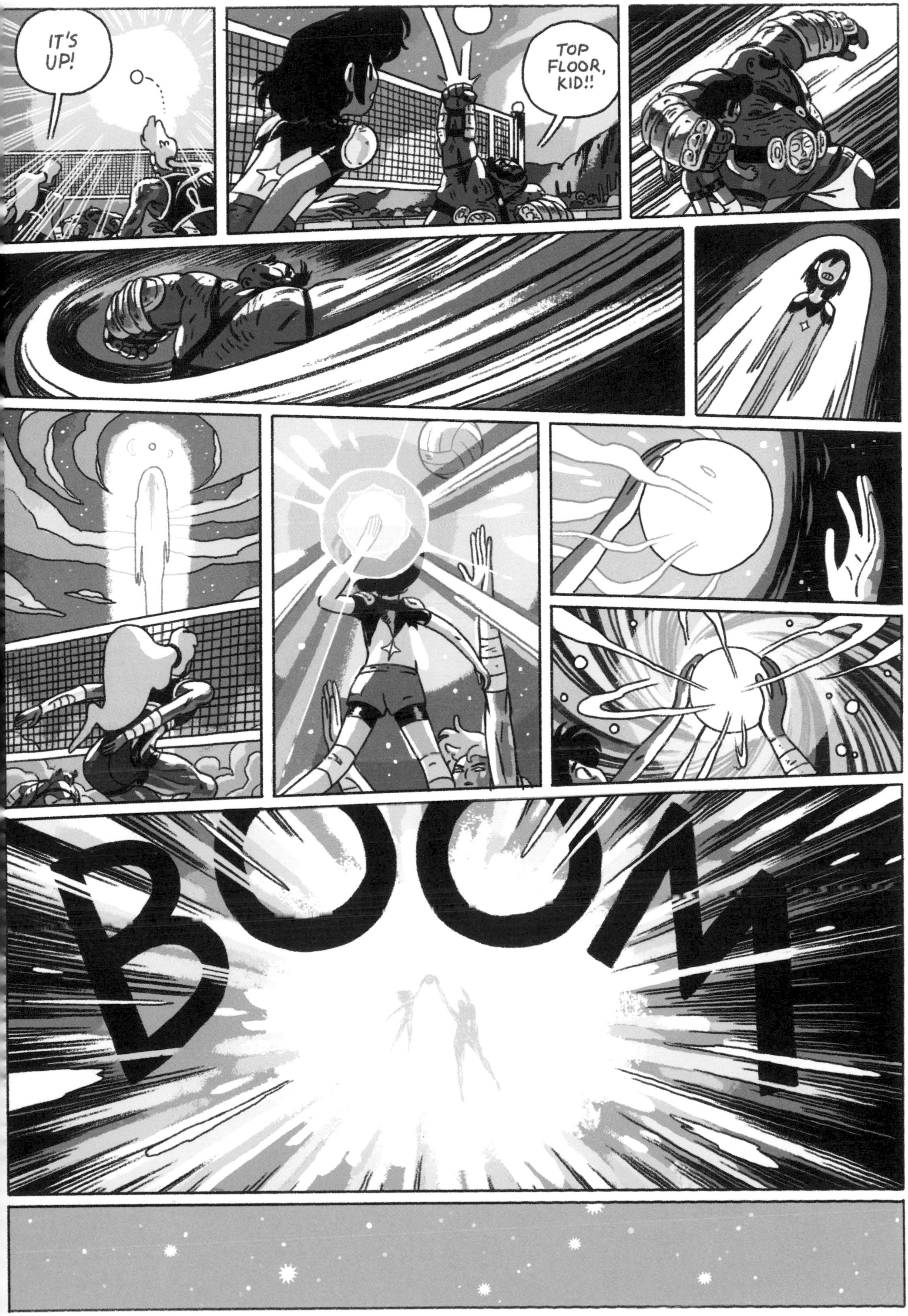
IT'S UP!
TOP FLOOR, KID!!
BOOM

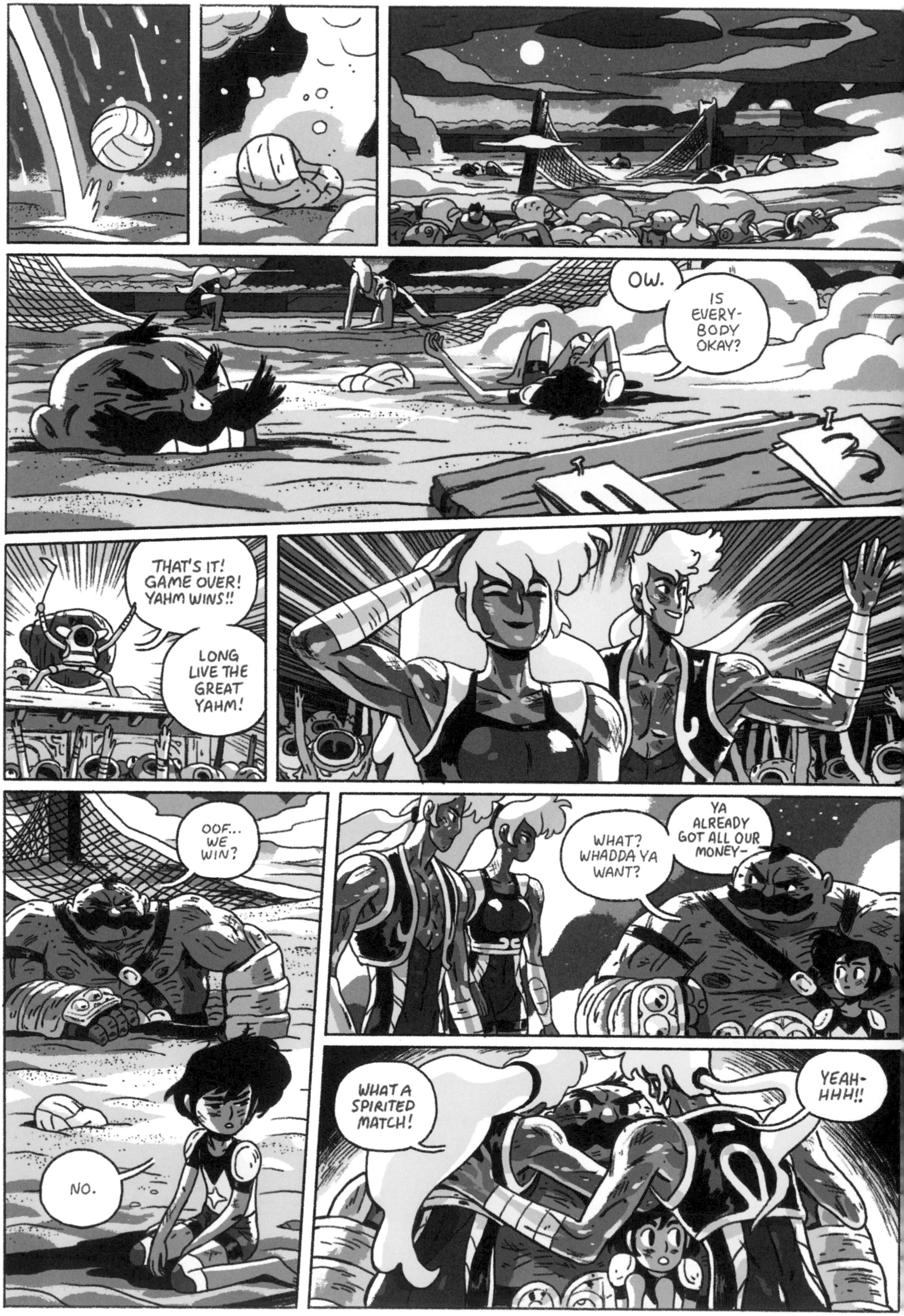
OW.
IS EVERY-BODY OKAY?
THAT'S IT! GAME OVER! YAHM WINS!!
LONG LIVE THE GREAT YAHM!
OOF... WE WIN?
NO.
WHAT? WHADDA YA WANT?
YA ALREADY GOT ALL OUR MONEY—
WHAT A SPIRITED MATCH!
YEAH-HHH!!

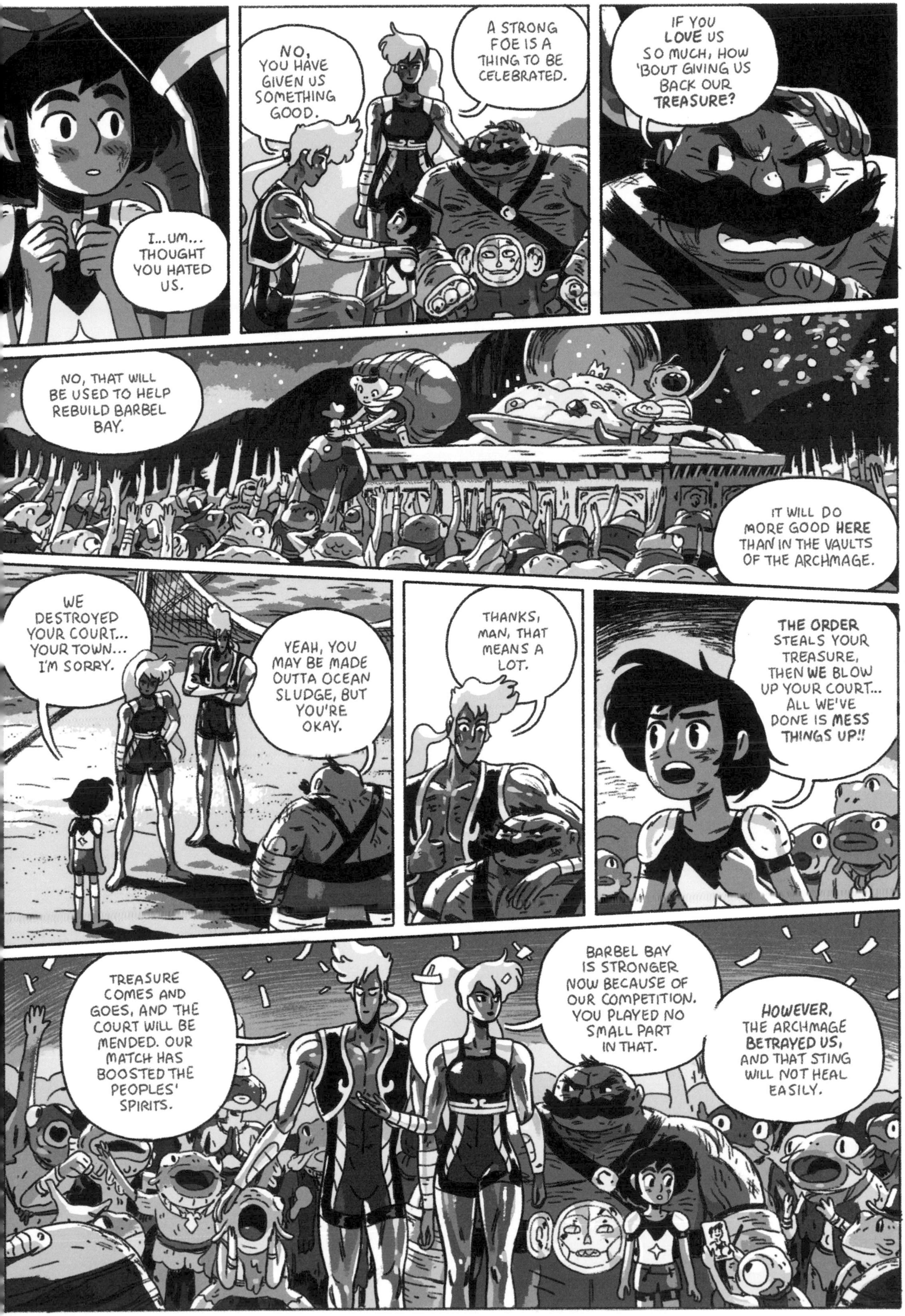
I...UM... THOUGHT YOU HATED US.
NO, YOU HAVE GIVEN US SOMETHING GOOD.
A STRONG FOE IS A THING TO BE CELEBRATED.
IF YOU LOVE US SO MUCH, HOW 'BOUT GIVING US BACK OUR TREASURE?
NO, THAT WILL BE USED TO HELP REBUILD BARBEL BAY.
IT WILL DO MORE GOOD HERE THAN IN THE VAULTS OF THE ARCHMAGE.
WE DESTROYED YOUR COURT... YOUR TOWN... I'M SORRY.
YEAH, YOU MAY BE MADE OUTTA OCEAN SLUDGE, BUT YOU'RE OKAY.
THANKS, MAN, THAT MEANS A LOT.
THE ORDER STEALS YOUR TREASURE, THEN WE BLOW UP YOUR COURT... ALL WE'VE DONE IS MESS THINGS UP!!
TREASURE COMES AND GOES, AND THE COURT WILL BE MENDED. OUR MATCH HAS BOOSTED THE PEOPLES' SPIRITS.
BARBEL BAY IS STRONGER NOW BECAUSE OF OUR COMPETITION. YOU PLAYED NO SMALL PART IN THAT.
HOWEVER, THE ARCHMAGE BETRAYED US, AND THAT STING WILL NOT HEAL EASILY.

BUT WHY? WHY WOULD THE ORDER ATTACK YOU GUYS.

THE ARCHMAGE HAS ALWAYS FEARED US.

SHE IS JEALOUS OF OUR POWER AND TEAMWORK.

YEAH, OKAY.

THE ORDER IS COVETOUS AS A BED OF SERPENTS.

HOARDING TREASURE AND SECRETS IN THAT BIG TRIANGLE.

FIRST, IT'S A PYRAMID.

SECOND, THE ORDER PROTECTS THAT STUFF 'CUZ IT'S DANGEROUS!

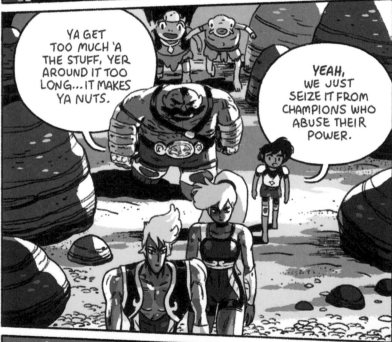

YA GET TOO MUCH 'A THE STUFF, YER AROUND IT TOO LONG... IT MAKES YA NUTS.

YEAH, WE JUST SEIZE IT FROM CHAMPIONS WHO ABUSE THEIR POWER.

LIKE US?

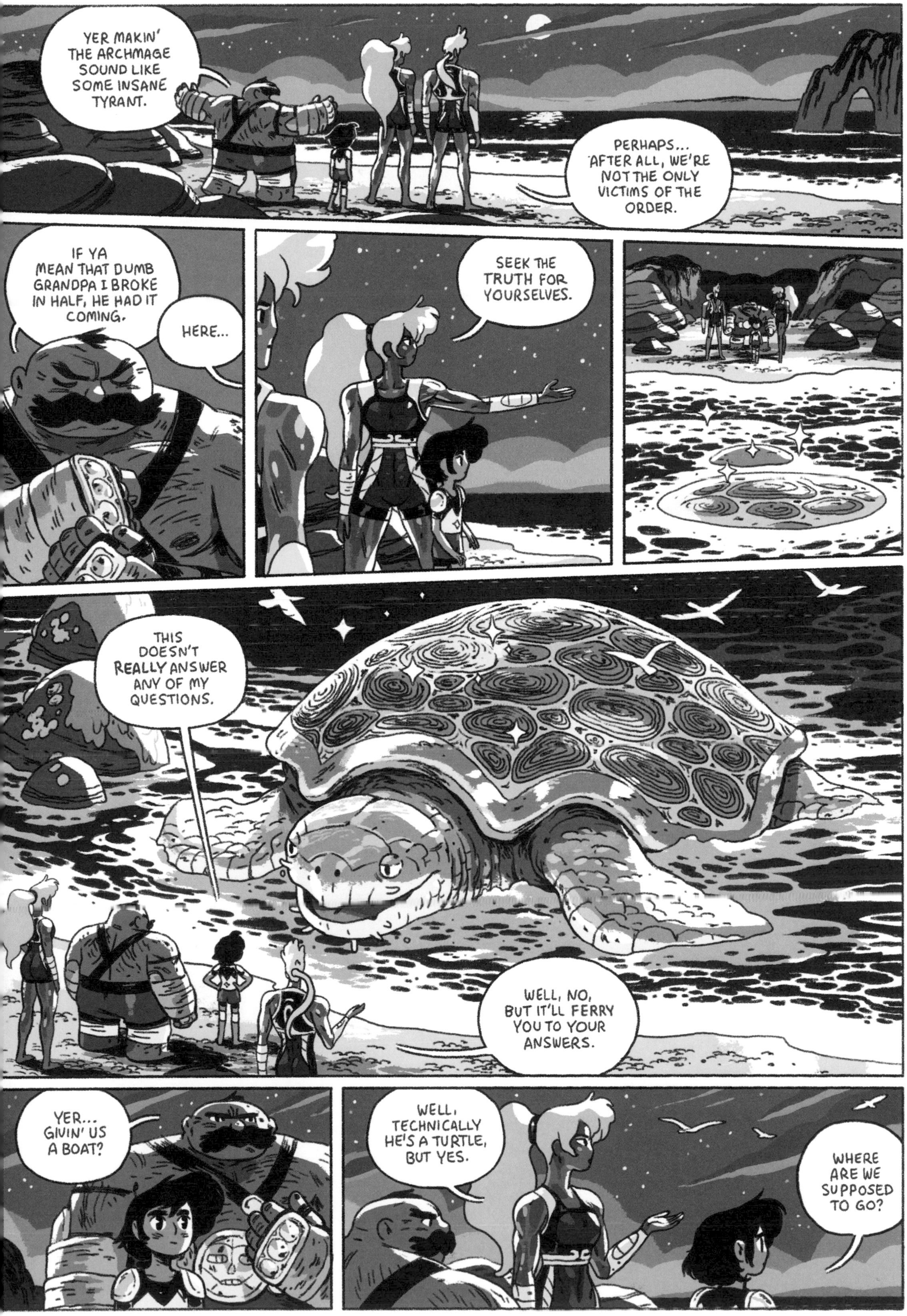
YER MAKIN' THE ARCHMAGE SOUND LIKE SOME INSANE TYRANT.
PERHAPS... AFTER ALL, WE'RE NOT THE ONLY VICTIMS OF THE ORDER.
IF YA MEAN THAT DUMB GRANDPA I BROKE IN HALF, HE HAD IT COMING.
HERE...
SEEK THE TRUTH FOR YOURSELVES.
THIS DOESN'T REALLY ANSWER ANY OF MY QUESTIONS.
WELL, NO, BUT IT'LL FERRY YOU TO YOUR ANSWERS.
YER... GIVIN' US A BOAT?
WELL, TECHNICALLY HE'S A TURTLE, BUT YES.
WHERE ARE WE SUPPOSED TO GO?

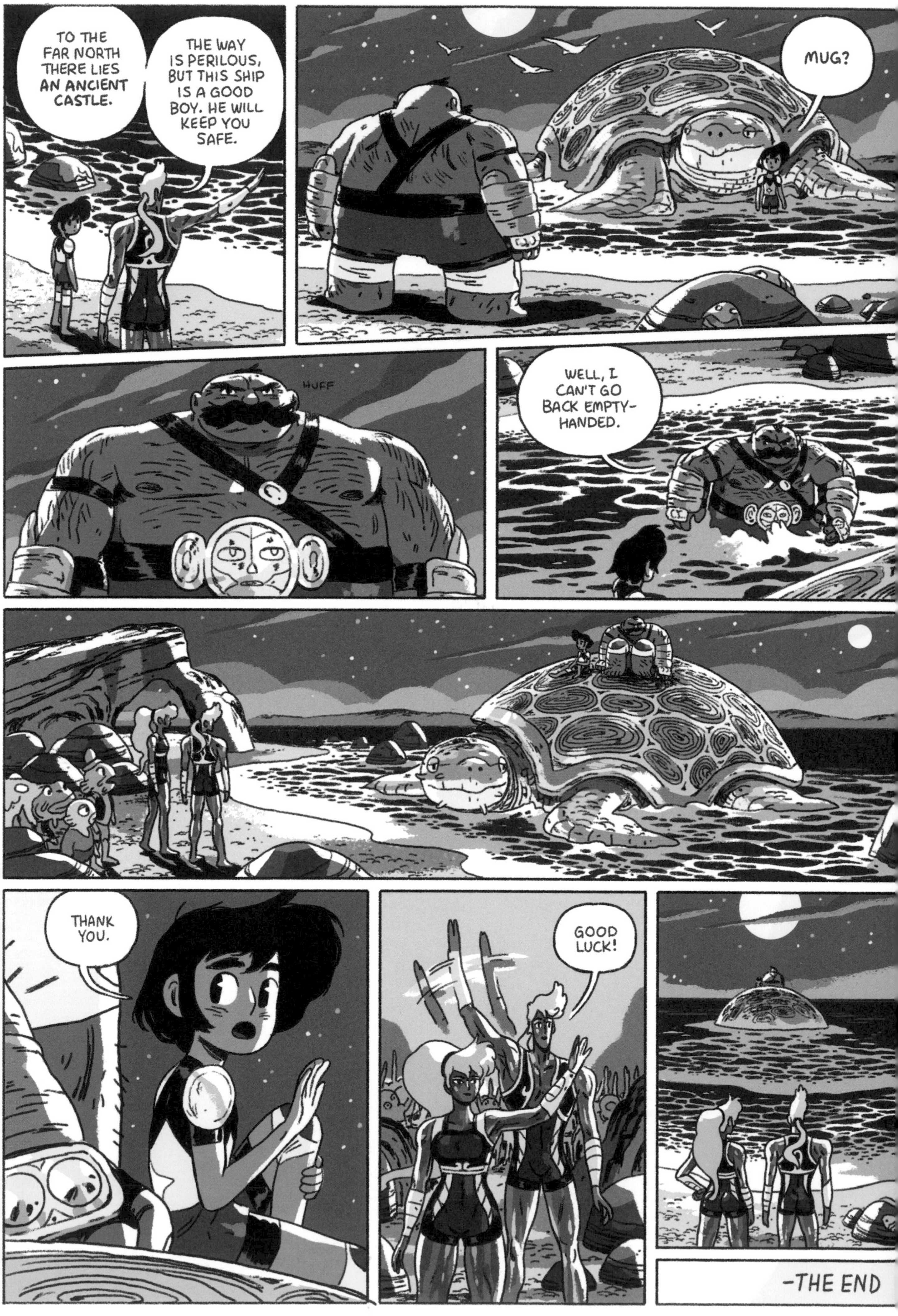
TO THE FAR NORTH THERE LIES AN ANCIENT CASTLE.
THE WAY IS PERILOUS, BUT THIS SHIP IS A GOOD BOY. HE WILL KEEP YOU SAFE.
MUG?
HUFF
WELL, I CAN'T GO BACK EMPTY-HANDED.
THANK YOU.
GOOD LUCK!
-THE END

F. S. III

COMING SOON...

FANTASY SPORTS N°2 IS © NOBROW 2016.

THIS IS A FIRST EDITION PUBLISHED IN 2016 BY
NOBROW LTD. 62 GREAT EASTERN STREET, LONDON, EC2A 3QR.

TEXT, CHARACTERS AND ILLUSTRATIONS © SAM BOSMA 2016.
SAM BOSMA HAS ASSERTED HIS RIGHT UNDER THE COPYRIGHT,
DESIGNS AND PATENTS ACT, 1988, TO BE IDENTIFIED AS THE AUTHOR OF THIS WORK.

PUBLISHED IN THE US BY NOBROW (US) INC.

PRINTED IN LATVIA ON FSC ASSURED PAPER.
ISBN: 978-1-910620-10-6

ORDER FROM WWW.NOBROW.NET

FSC
www.fsc.org

MIX
Paper from
responsible sources
FSC® C002795

DORADO
ZIM